RAINBOW CRYSTAL

SAMANTHA CAPRIO-NEGRET

Dear Isabella,
Keep believing in your
dreams, in magic, &
That anything is possible!
Ride on unicorns
our rainbows!!
Best,
J. Caprio-Negret
xox

Rainbow Crystal
by Samantha Caprio-Negret
Published by Clean Reads
www.cleanreads.com

In loving memory of my soul sister and best friend forever ∼ JLB ∼ until we meet again and have many more magical adventures together.

PROLOGUE

There's no question that the psychic was right about something significant happening to me and my best friend, but I never imagined this.

Josie Lee lies lifeless on the hospital bed. Her hands are blue-purple in color. It's so freaky. The only thing that remains of my best friend is heavy breathing, which the machine is doing for her. My eyes roam the freezing, unfamiliar ICU room. Quivers bolt down my whole body as I watch her chest rise and fall, and I can feel the tiny little goose-bump raise hairs on my arms. Even though her eyes are closed and aren't ever going to open again, I move her blonde hair away from them, away from all the tubes. *How does that even do that? And how could this happen?* I fidget then bite a loose piece of cuticle from my thumb.

Her body took a beating from the car that hit her and took off. It was around eight o'clock at night on Sunday, January 28th. Now, I will never forget that date, and that phone call we got last night from her mom. My body shakes as I remember the screaming and crying on the other end.

The police came in asking Josie Lee's mom questions. After

they left, I noticed the police report placed on the side of the hospital bed. So, I took a little peek. I read it with one eye open, even though I didn't want to, but did at the same time. My parents told me that I was too young to understand. *Is ten-years-old too young?* But, I feel like I understand what's going on. But really, I just understand Josie Lee better than anyone. There's no one else who understands us; who understands our rare friendship. *So there!* We're soul sisters, and we knew it when we first met.

I grab hold of Josie Lee's hand tight, but there's no response, and know there will never be one again, but I can still wish. Josie Lee's eyes remain shut and sunken in, and her skin is as pale as a ghost. That's what she is now...just a ghost. Gone. Brain-dead. It's just a shell of a body that's left. The hospital will have to pull the plug soon. More chills run up and down my spine.

The report stated the car that hit her tossed her like fifty feet in the air, and she landed on someone's driveway. I hope it didn't hurt her too bad. It's too awful to even imagine. I bite my lower lip and fight back the tears.

The car left at first, but then turned around and came back. The driver said he thought a brick hit his car. *What an idiot. Was he blind or something?* The police just wrote the guy a speeding ticket. *Other idiots.* In the report, witnesses driving from the other direction said that they saw the whole thing take place. They stopped their car and got out. Apparently, hovering over Josie Lee's body was a young blonde-haired boy, attempting to help her. By the time they got to Josie Lee's side, the boy was nowhere to be found. They first thought the boy had left flowers there because they got this strong smell of gardenias or roses or something around. *Weird.* Because, I've been smelling the same thing a lot lately too.

I feel a light tap on the back of my shoulder. Without saying a word, I turn around and look down at what appears to be a short nurse who reaches just above my waist in height. Her golden, wavy hair flows loosely and bounces above her shoulders. I whiff what smells like freshly-baked cookies. *Mmm... that's different.* The nurse's eyes sparkle blue when she hands me a folded letter with a light shade of glittery-pink fingernails.

It's some sort of old, out-dated paper. I lift the shimmering seal to reveal these words.

From Raiven:

Now that your wish has been made and granted, upon a shooting star~

   There's an important quest at hand, no need to look too far.
   It's time for you—the chosen one—to come along~
   And don't be alarmed, for it won't be very long.

There are those hairs on my arms again, standing up. A scattering sound distracts me. I look up from the letter to ask the nurse who this is from, but she's nowhere to be seen. The little nurse disappears as quickly as she appeared. *What or who is Raiven? What, "won't be very long?" Strange. Oh well!* But, that's not even the strangest thing. Lately, there's been too many to explain. That is a weird coincidence about a wish, though. I remember it. But, it's not important right now. My best friend is about to die... that's all that matters to me. *Good grief!* I really can't stop quivering, so I rub friction up and down my arms with both hands. A kid in school taught me how to do that—makes you feel heat on your skin.

Suddenly, I feel a cold rush in the room like someone else has come in. The lingering smell of cookies starts to turn more flower-like. It gets stronger and stronger. I raise my nose high in the air and breathe in. There it is again. *The smell is amazing!* Like gardenias. I know what gardenias smell like because my mother has a gardenia bush growing outside of our house, but also because I've smelt it before...a bunch of times. It seems to be following me around more than usual lately. But, I've smelled it my whole life, almost like it's always been there. *What is going on?*

Did anyone else in the room even notice that nurse hand me a letter? I cram it in the pocket of my jeans. Josie Lee's parents don't seem to take notice to any of it. *Again, strange.*

Penny, Josie Lee's mom, stands on the other end of the bed, crying and rubbing her daughter's bruised head. My heart aches for her. You can see she really loves her only child. Even though she's a bit quirky, she's a good person. Her rules never really made any sense to me—like Josie Lee couldn't use a tablet at the dinner table, yet she could call boys on the phone. *My parents would never!*

I look at her and don't know what else to do, so I deliver her a slight smile. It feels fake, a little awkward. *What do I say in a time like this?* My eyes roam around the room, and they land on her father who just sits there in the chair, ankle crossed over his knee, waiting with roaming eyes and a jumpy leg. *What could he possibly be staring at besides his daughter?*

I feel sick to my stomach and can't even look at him, so I look up at the ceiling. *Is that splattered blood up there? Eww!* I tremble. If Josie Lee wouldn't have gotten into an argument with her father, she wouldn't have stormed out of the house last night. She wouldn't have been walking in the dark on the side of the street, and the car wouldn't have hit her. Josie Lee is always being let down by her father; she never felt like she existed in his world. I know because she told me that. And even almost dead, she still wasn't getting that love and attention. *I could just punch him!* My fist clenches up.

How could he not see that beautiful girl that I see? I'll never forget that sunny day I met Josie Lee on the swing at the park in my new backyard. That smile that lights up a room. I will always remember it. She always knew how to make me feel like a better person. When we first met, she told me how special and beautiful I was. She befriended me right away without conditions. Only girl who ever did that. Every time we hung out, it was like the first time all over again. She had a way about her that somehow let me know I was one of the most important people in the world to her.

I felt so alone and scared in a new city, and never thought I'd meet any friends who would like me. Then all of a sudden...*poof!* Josie Lee was the first and coolest girl I ever met; besides the fact that she always had the funkiest nail art, like light purple with black polka-a-dots, or something like that.

And just as my thoughts begin to fade back to that first day in my new home—that same day I met her— I see it there...sitting on the end railing of her hospital bed. It takes shape into a small ball of sparkling, glowing, glittery-light. It gets bigger and bigger, forming into a...*a fairy?* It's not like I've ever seen a fairy in person before, but I know what a fairy looks like, and it's a fairy alright...*a young blonde-haired fairy boy*. The smell of gardenias is overbearing. I rub my eyes with both fists to get a better view. *Am I dreaming?*

CHAPTER ONE

A New Best Friend

THE BEDROOM DOOR swings open and the light switch turns on. I sit up in my bed, aching with agitation. "What? Why did you turn my light on? I'm sleeping."

Tiana Rose, my older sister, is standing in my doorway with a goofy, child-like grin on her face. "I just wanted to see if you were awake."

"Well, obviously, you can see I'm not, so please leave me alone," I mumble as I pull the covers up over my head.

"Come on, Seraphina. Mom's making pancakes for us. Don't you want some?"

"I'm still sleeping!" I jump up from under my covers, throwing a small pillow at Tiana Rose. It smacks her in the face. "Shut my door!"

Tiana Rose's glasses dangle and barely hang onto the tip of her nose.

The door slams behind her as her elephant-like footsteps

pound away in the distance. "She's sleeping, Mom. Don't wake her up, ok. She's sleeping. She doesn't want pancakes, Mom. Don't bother her, ok, because she's sleeping and is really cranky."

I lie there in bed trying to doze back to sleep. For a brief second, I do feel guilty about doing that to my sister with special needs. But, I can't help how annoying she can be at times, and I just don't have the patience for her right now.

The irritating sound of a lawn mower blasts outside my bedroom window. I toss and turn under the covers trying to get comfortable again, but it's useless. "Ugh! What does a person have to do to get some sleep around here? *Fine!* I guess I'll get up and have some pancakes then."

I stumble into my new bathroom, yawn, and take a glimpse of myself in the mirror. My hair looks like I stuck my finger into an electrical socket, and my pink, cotton nightgown slips off my shoulder. "Wow! This is cute. Maybe this is how I should go out today in my new neighborhood to make friends – just how I am."

I stick my pasty-white tongue out at myself in the mirror. "Eww. Whew-wee." Smacking my lips together, I pack some toothpaste on my toothbrush.

After I brush, I get one last glance at myself in the mirror to get a good look at my freshly-brushed, white teeth. "Ah, now that's more like it."

I slouch into the kitchen, passing by the unopened boxes all over the house from the move. My dad and Tiana Rose are sitting at the dining table. Tiana Rose stuffs pancakes in her mouth, while my dad reads a newspaper. Probably the only person in the world who still does. My mom is cooking more pancakes and pours a glass of orange juice. I pull out a chair and take a seat at the table.

My dad peeks behind his newspaper to look at me with a big

grin on his face. "Good morning, Squirt. How did you sleep? It's a beautiful, sunny Florida morning, huh?"

"Yeah, I guess." My dad sure is peppy this morning. *Ugh.* I pile two pancakes on my plate and lather them with maple syrup, taking a minute before I dig in. I'm not giving away my joy about eating them to my parents just yet.

My mom joins us. "Eat up." She points to the pancakes, then looks at me. "I made them especially for you and your sister. I know how you guys *love* your pancakes."

I examine Tiana Rose stuffing them in her mouth, not even making room for air.

"Take your time, sweetie." My mom says to her. "Mommy doesn't want you to choke."

Tiana Rose finishes her stack of pancakes before I can even take a bite of one of my own. My unfinished plate almost gets swiped up from me.

"Stop it! I haven't even touched mine yet." I slap Tiana Rose's hand away. Sometimes, I feel like the older sister.

My mom grasps Tiana Rose's arm gently. "Honey, sit back down, other people aren't done eating yet."

Tiana Rose immediately sits back down, then picks up her earphones lying on the dining table and puts them over her head. No one else in the world has an original with basic stations, but my mom has to find her that kind because that's all she can figure out how to use. A new set comes in about every couple of months, being she always accidentally breaks them.

I watch as Tiana Rose changes the channel over and over again till she finally settles on something. I can't tell what song she's trying to sing, because it sounds more like a cow in agony; there isn't any harmony in her voice, yet she seems like she couldn't care less. She doesn't understand other people's judgments of her. To me, this is more of a blessing than a curse.

There must be such a feeling of complete freedom that comes with that.

Her lips smack together to take breaks in between verses. *Smack, smack, smack.*

The singing and humming out of tune pierces my ears, and I cover them with my hands. "Can someone please stop her? That's terrible."

My mom starts laughing. "I think it's hilarious."

"Yeah, *real* funny, Mom. More like *hideous,* instead of *hilarious.*"

"Oh, stop it. Just focus on something else, ok?"

My dad, still reading the newspaper, takes a sip of his coffee. "Squirt, listen to your mom, ok?" He puts the newspaper down on the table to fix himself a plate. His hair has that wet, gelled-back look, and he smells of spice cologne. This is the scent he's had my whole life, and it's still my favorite, even when he's aggravating me. It doesn't matter whether he's in a suit and tie or T-shirt and shorts, he's wearing it. Taking a deep inhale, I turn my head so he won't notice. I'm still completely furious that he made me move here to this hot and humid place because of a dumb job offer.

"How does a person go from running a deli in New Jersey to doing real estate in South Florida? Makes no sense." I ask while chewing on a piece of food.

It's clear with the look he shoots me he senses attitude. "I told you already. Before you girls, I lived down here. I'm from here. Your mom is from New Jersey. When she became pregnant, I moved there for her to start a family. My siblings are down here, and when my brothers asked me to do real estate with them, it seemed like the ideal thing to do, and we wanted to start a new chapter. Running the deli was a hard lifestyle." He replies as his eyebrows crinkle.

"Most people feel blessed to live here. They say it's paradise.

So, why don't you go outside and make some new friends? Play in the park in the back. Get your mind on something positive." My dad takes a bite of pancakes, and then he looks at my mom and smiles; his dimple deepens. Usually I think it's one of his best features, but at this moment in time, it irks me to no end. It's probably because he ruined my life. "Ok, Dad, whatever." I roll my eyes at him.

My mom takes a long sip of coffee. After what seems to be the longest pause in history, she turns to face me. "I know you miss your friends and New Jersey, but you'll like it here eventually. It's going to take some getting used to. Once you start school, you'll meet a lot of new friends. Try and look at the brighter side of things…it's all about *attitude*. Plus, we have to support your dad's new job."

Easy for my mom to say. She doesn't have to start a new school or meet new friends. Plus, she has my dad. Boys are a *whole* other story. I know that my parents have been married for like ever.

"Great! I'm *so thrilled* to go play in a park in this heat." I swallow my pancakes to bite a loose piece of cuticle from my thumb. "I'm not a baby anymore, guys."

"Hey!" My dad raises his voice. "Now, be nice, Squirt, we're just trying to help you here. And we're not 'guys'…we're your parents. You'll meet new friends; now stop acting like a baby if you're not." I slump over my plate. There's that Italian temper that I've grown to know and love. *They just don't get it.*

"You both don't have to be faced with new kids at a new school, picking on you. I always had some girl at school wanting to beat me up for some unknown reason. I just got that bully off my case back home, and now I'll have to start all over again." My lips start to tremble as I speak, I can feel it. *No. Don't be a cry-baby.*

My mom reaches out and brushes her fingers along the side

of my face to push my hair aside. "Sweetie, that's because they're jealous of you. You'll always be faced with that wherever you go. It's something you'll have to just deal with. Trust me, I know this from experience." She shakes her head, and her bobbed dark-brown hair springs around her pretty hazel eyes and tan skin.

I push my mom's hand out of the way. I squirm and position my back against my chair, then fold my arms, still not touching my food. "I don't understand. Why in the world would anyone be jealous of *me*? I'm no one special."

"Oh, you're not, huh?" My mom responds. "When I was pregnant with you, I just knew you were meant to be special. Right, honey?" She looks at my dad. "Tell your daughter."

I watch as the same hand that just brushed my face a minute ago is now placed on my dad's hand that rests on the table.

"Your mom's right. We always knew that you were a gift from God because you were...well, let's just say...a pleasant surprise." My dad takes a loud slurp of coffee and then smiles. "We didn't want to have any more children after your sister, not that that's *her* fault. It's just that we had a lot of responsibility weighing in on us with taking care of a child with special needs; it's been rough. You brought so much light into our house after you were born. So, you are our shining star, kid." He winks.

I start to have a warm and fuzzy moment, but then the reality of the situation clicks back into my mind. "I still don't understand how that would make kids at school jealous of me?" *Uh-oh. Your voice is getting chocked up. See? You are just a big baby.*

"Because, honey, you're beautiful *and* smart," my mom says with a smirk. "Most importantly, you've got a good heart; people will try and bring you down for that. They're intimidated by you. If you could, honey, you'd put a bandage on the world to heal it."

"What?" I ask. "How can people be mean to you because you're a *good person*? How does that make any sense?"

"That's because of the person you are, Seraphina," my dad says, "not everyone on the planet is like you. There are some good people, and there are some evil people. Remember, there is *always* a battle in the world between the two."

I grow even more frustrated and confused with what my parents are saying, so I start biting my cuticles.

"It's ok, honey," my mom says. "You don't have to understand all of this now. You're still very young. You'll get it one day."

"Well, I guess you're right about that; some people just like being straight out mean and cruel. I've seen some kids before make fun of Tiana Rose, and I don't understand how you can do that to someone who's different."

The memory of me throwing the pillow at Tiana Rose scatters through my head, and I cringe inside. Sometimes I can lose my patience with her because living with her can be difficult, and I feel like running away. It's not an excuse. I'm not proud of it; it's a trait that I need to work on. That, and biting my cuticles, I think as I notice myself doing it. *Stop.*

Tiana Rose is bobbling her head and snapping her pudgy fingers to the music. Her tune still completely out of harmony. This time I can't help but smile at my sister's innocence.

"Unfortunately, you will witness that in your life," my dad says. "But, you always stick to who you really are, what you believe in, and don't ever try and be anyone that you're not—especially to impress someone else."

"Yes, Daddy." I crack a little bit of a smile.

"See, there's my shining star I know and love." My dad smiles back at me; his dimples beam with delight.

≈

I SKIP on over to the park my parents were talking about earlier. I see the public swing set, run over to it, and plop myself down on one of the swings. Feeling the need to be free for a moment, I pull my body swiftly back and then forward until I gather up enough speed and strength to swing myself high up in the air.

I hate the thought of having to make new friends. So, the only thing I can think to do is pray. *Dear God, please help me find a new friend here in Florida that I like and who likes me back. I feel so alone. I miss my home in New Jersey and my friends. Why did we have to move to this stupid place?* Even my prayer turns into a rant. I can't concentrate. But, I know I have to try and at least do what my parents said...something about having a positive attitude.

I squint my eyes and lift my face to the sun, focusing on the feeling of my hair blowing in the wind. Back and forth, back and forth, I swing higher and higher. Every time I come back down, I get a huge rush from my stomach dropping. *So exhilarating!*

Then, out of nowhere, my happiness is interrupted by a cheerful girl's voice. "Hey, can I join you here? Looks like you're having too much fun alone."

I open my eyes to see a pretty, blonde, blue-eyed girl point to the empty swing next to me. Slowing down on my swing, I examine the girl wearing short cut-off jean shorts with a black and white T-shirt that reads *Rockstar*. Her lips are a perfect heart-shaped red and a light-brown mole sits right above them. She seems different, unique.

"Well?" The blonde girl stares at me with her hands on her hips. "Can I join you or what? Is anyone sitting here?" She points to the empty swing next to me and flickers her mascara-applied, long eyelashes. I also couldn't help but take notice of her neon, yellow nail polish color.

I observe a little gap between her two front teeth. In some weird way, it looks ok on her. Not ugly.

"Umm...no...I mean...yes, you can join me, if you like. No one is sitting there." At this point, my swing is at a total stop.

"Thanks. I thought you'd never ask," the blonde says and smiles.

I stare at her, frozen. There is something about her, but I can't quite put my finger on it. *Hmm?* She is pretty, but that's not it.

The girl offers her hand for me to shake. "Hi, my name is Josie Lee. What's yours?"

I extend out my hand to shake hers back, but wipe it on the sleeve of my shirt first because my palm is sweaty. Not sure if it's from being so hot or from nerves. "Oh, hi, my name is Seraphina."

"Seraphina, huh? That's different." She begins swinging, slowly picking up speed. "What does it mean?"

It breaks my trance, and I realize I'm still not moving, so I pick up the speed again. "I don't know. I never really thought about it before," I answer Josie Lee's strange question. *Is she always this straight forward?*

"Really?" Josie Lee asks. "Well, you should know what it means, or at least to know who you're named after."

"Well, what does your name mean?" I ask. *Ha. Gotcha now.*

"Well, I know I was named after that famous actress, Jamie Lee Curtis. But my mom liked the way that Josie sounded. She says it has more of a ring to it."

"I don't get it," I respond.

Josie Lee rolls her eyes. "I know. Doesn't really make any sense, but then again, neither does my mom."

There's a moment of silence.

I shift in my swing, trying to get comfortable and avoid the little bit of awkward silence. But, she does seem like an interesting person. I'm not sure if it's her, I don't-seem-to-care attitude, funky way she dresses, or that she's wearing make-up at our age, but she's definitely different in comparison to other girls I've met before, and it's not exactly like I have any other friends at the moment. Most of the girls I usually meet seem just plain, boring, and ordinary. Nothing about them ever stands out. But, *this* girl, I can tell...it's just a feeling.

"You're new here, huh?" Josie Lee asks.

I look at her, slouching in my swing. "Y..yeah. How did you know?"

"I know a new face when I see one. I'm at this park all the time, and pretty much know all the faces in this neighborhood. I definitely would've remembered you."

I can feel myself blush. "We actually moved here yesterday."

"Well, welcome to the neighborhood." Josie Lee smiles and picks up speed. "Are you going to go to school at Visionary Middle in the fall?"

"No, I'm only going into fifth grade," I reply. "Is that the school you go to?" Inside, I'm hoping it isn't, being this is the only person I will know there, and so far, she seems to be pretty nice and super cool.

Josie Lee swings her whole body, looking like she's about to do a back flip in the air, but doesn't. "Yeah. I start sixth grade there soon. I could have sworn you were my age. I'll be eleven in December. You?"

"I turn ten this September." At least it's not too far away, making me feel a bit older.

"I heard it's a cool school. I'm excited. I heard there's some pretty cute boys there." Josie Lee winks.

I hang my head down slightly, feeling nervousness in my

belly. The fact she's thinking about boys already scares the crap out of me. "I'm just looking to make new friends," I hesitate for a second, "and well, I guess just fit in. I don't know anyone here. It's a little scary." That just blurted out.

Josie Lee looks at me with her head tilted to one side, and her swing begins slowing until it comes to a complete stop. I'm not sure what she's going to say or do, so I copy her.

She grabs my hand and gazes into my eyes. "Well, you've already made one. So, don't you worry. You just stick with me, and you'll be fine." After granting me another wink, she pulls me up from the swing without releasing my hand. "Come... let's take a walk." Feeling like a little lost puppy, I follow her.

I release my hand from hers to wipe the sweat beads that are tickling the top of my lip. After viewing the neighboring homes that line up behind the park for blocks, I wonder which one of them is Josie Lee's house. *Where did she come from?* We walk the black, cement-paved sidewalk and continue our conversation.

"I like you, Seraphina, there's something special about you. I feel like I know you from somewhere. I have this strange feeling that we've met before."

That's how I feel, but I'm still curious. "What do you mean, 'met before?' I just moved here. How could we have met before?" I rub the bottom of my chin.

Josie Lee waves her hand. "Not in this lifetime, silly. We've been together in past lives."

Ok. That's one I've definitely never heard before. "What? 'Past lives?' How do you know that? What lifetime?" I'm scrambling to find the right words, ask the proper questions. *So, what to do next?*

"You sure ask a lot of questions, don't you?" She laughs. "You shouldn't do that to your fingers, it's a bad habit." She glances at my finger in my mouth. "I mean, look at what you're doing to your poor fingers. Plus, it's not very pretty, and you are."

"Oh," I throw my finger out of my mouth. I'm not sure if I'm blushing. My cheeks burn a bit. It's probably just from the scorching sun. I examine my ugly, chewed-up cuticles. "Yeah, nervous habit. Sorry."

"Anyway, I don't necessarily know that we've been together in past lives, but it's just a strong feeling I have." Josie Lee's hands wave as if she's conducting an orchestra. It's when you meet someone for the first time, and you get this funny feeling that you've met them already, it means that you've probably known them in a past life. So, we were supposed to meet again in this life." She has a big grin on her face while explaining.

"I've read about it in this book at this really cool metaphysical store I go to. I'll take you there sometime. You'll love it."

"What's a meta-what-store?" I ask. I must sound dumb saying that.

Josie Lee giggles. She swats the side of my arm. Oh, silly. "It's a store filled with all these treasures—like crystals, stones, and statues of fairies. It's awesome!"

"Wow!" I say. "Sounds awesome. Sure. I would love to go."

A very colorful butterfly flies past us. *Hmm?* Never seen one with that many colors before. She nudges my shoulder with her own, disrupting my thoughts. "Well, don't you have that feeling? Like we've met already?" she pesters.

I bust out with, "I guess," shrugging my shoulders.

"I wonder what we were previously...maybe sisters?" Josie Lee gawks up at the sky, almost like her answers are coming from up above. "Yeah, kind of feels like we were sisters together in a past life."

What is she looking at? And where is she getting this stuff from?

I have to think about this for a minute. I mean, I do

somehow feel comfortable with her already, and we did only meet about a half hour ago. "Yeah, you're actually right. I guess it does," I respond.

"See, we're best friends already then?" She asks, putting her arm around me.

I really like the sound of that. Seems as if God is answering my prayers after all. *Wow. A new, best friend.*

"More like soul sisters." She squeezes me harder.

Even though I hesitate a bit, it does sound cool enough. Plus, I really like her, and I can tell she really likes me too. *So, why not?* "Yeah. Sure. Soul sisters."

From a short distance away, I notice a small figure from behind a tree glance at us and disappear. I smell a trace of gardenia flowers.

THE MEMORIES FADE OUT, and my thoughts come back to the here and now present reality. I'm staring at this ball of light, which has now become a small fairy boy. Yes, a fairy. I mean, he has wings, and they're sparkling. His peach skin looks like it's lathered in glitter. *Is this really happening?* I think, rubbing my eyes.

This fairy boy smiles at me and points in the direction to Josie Lee's lifeless body. I glance back at her, and I see a big poof of air lift her hospital gown. Out of it, floats up a gleaming girl with long, blonde, flowing hair and a soft, delicate, white gown to match, which twinkles and glows all of these rainbow colors. It's like she stepped out of her own body. She's happy and seems fine, and she beckons me to follow her. There's a sense of peacefulness in the air.

I look back at the fairy boy, and he nods in her direction. His arms are now folded behind his back.

Josie Lee's mom continues to rub her head, and her dad is now reading a magazine. I have to close my mouth so no one notices my shock. But, nobody else in the room sees this but me. Josie Lee's mom doesn't look away for a minute from her, and her father's face is covered by whatever unimportant crap he's bothering reading.

The girl is Josie Lee. No doubt it's her. She's still waving her hand for me to follow her and moving toward the wall of the hospital room. *Is she going to go through it? What? But, how?*

"Seraphina?" Someone grabs my arm from behind me.

"What?" I thrash my body around to see my mom. *When did she come into the room?*

"Seraphina. We have to go now. We've been sitting outside in the waiting room for you. The doctor told me to come get you. It's time, honey. I'm sorry. You have to say your final goodbyes."

The only thing that keeps me from doing so is my memories of her. I can't help but jump back into them. This reality is too hard to bear.

CHAPTER TWO

_____

Seal the Deal

WHEN I OPEN my front door, I notice my best friend, Josie Lee, has something strange under her arm. *What now?*

With a big grin on her face she says, "You can talk to spirits on it." She hands me some sort of a board-game that you can communicate to dead people with, and then nudges me out of the way.

Josie Lee walks straight into my bedroom, and she plops down on my floor, sitting Indian-style. She flips her blonde hair to one side and opens up her hands to me. "Well? Are you going to come join me or just stare at me with that weird look on your face?"

I follow her and walk over to it. "Yeah. I know what it is…and only coo-coo birds play this. Really, Josie Lee?"

"I thought it would be fun to try it out," she says with a big, goofy smirk.

"You and your supernatural stuff that you love. You're

crazy." I say as I sit down, copying her style, and tearing open the wrapper to the new game.

Josie Lee giggles. "Yeah, and you love it too; don't lie."

I didn't want to admit it to her, but I did deep down inside. My heart races and my palms sweat.

I lay down the board and the weird thing-a-ma-jig that moves over the letters facing me; our fingers meet in the middle touching it. I notice she has our favorite dark-red nail polish color on, which is starting to chip.

It slowly starts to move. The hair on my arms stands up.

I slap Josie Lee's hand off of the moving object, looking at her spooked. "You're moving it, come on."

She tosses both hands up in the air. "I swear...I'm not doing it." Her blue eyes bulge from her face while her hands flow with the motion of the moving object that slides across the board. "This thing is so cool. Why haven't I done this before?"

I notice Josie Lee's body rocking; she can barely contain herself. "Come on. Ask it something, Seraphina."

"What do you want me to ask it? You ask it something."

"Fine, chicken." Josie Lee looks at me. "Are you a spirit?"

The eerie moving object, with both of our hands still placed gently on top, moves to the *Yes* response.

After a short pause, I ask, "Are you a male or female?"

It slowly goes to the *M*, then the *A*, then the *L*, and stops, landing on the *E*.

I shudder. "Crazy."

Then Josie Lee asks it with a loud voice in slow motion, "Are you someone who one of us knows?"

Again, it moves to the *Yes*.

Josie Lee throws her hands off of it. Next, she grabs a pillow from my bed, and hits me on the side of the head with it.

"Ouch! What was that for?" I ask, rubbing the spot on my head where she hit me.

"Ok, let's stop. It's starting to get spooky." Josie Lee throws the game off to the side. "You're scared. I can see it written all over your face."

"Oh, really?" I ask with my arms folded, realizing Josie Lee is trying to put the blame on me, because she doesn't want to admit *she* is actually the scared one. "Well, isn't that the point?"

I sit there staring at Josie Lee serious for a few seconds. My hair feels all messed up from the pillow attack a minute ago. Plus, my head is still throbbing.

Josie Lee holds her belly from the laughter. So, I decide to take one of my pillows sitting next to her and come back with a slam to her head, taking Josie Lee by surprise. She holds her hand to the side of her head with her mouth hanging open. "You didn't just do that?"

"Oh, yes I did! Gotcha back! You can dish it, but you can't take it, huh? Hurts, doesn't it?"

Now we both are laughing and hitting each other as hard as we can with the pillows, turning it into a full-blown, fun pillow fight. It ends with us standing up on my bed.

"Ok, stop, stop. You're making me laugh too hard; I can't take it anymore. I need a break." She bends down to take a sip from her glass of orange juice.

I make funny faces at Josie Lee, so that when she goes to take a sip, she can't swallow it. The orange juice spits out everywhere from her mouth—some of it even comes out through her nose.

I laugh so hard tears are streaming down my face. "Ok, sorry, I'll stop." I sigh deeply trying to get myself together; Josie Lee copies.

We both plop back down on the bed and face each other. "You are so funny...and so beautiful." Josie Lee says. "It's not fair."

"Come on. You're pretty too...and funny. I wish I was as

outgoing and fearless as you are. You're not afraid of anything. I'm a wimp. Plus, I'm ordinary, with boring brown eyes and brown hair." I toss my long, thick hair away from my shoulder. "Look at you. You've got pretty blonde hair, blue eyes, and are already getting boobs." I can't believe I said that to her.

Josie Lee looks at me and makes a huge funny-looking grin. "Nah. You just haven't come out of your shell yet. You'd be surprised; you have that inner strength and confidence that's just waiting to come out and shine. But, don't worry, that's what I'm here for. Plus, I'm a year older than you, so I'm just a little more experienced." She shoots me a wink. She loves to do that. I think she thinks it makes her seem older or something.

"You know, you're the only real friend I've ever had." I've never opened up to anyone like that before, but I feel close enough to share this with her. We've been best friends now for about four months since I moved to Florida.

"Same with me. You're the first *real* best friend I've ever had too." Josie Lee tilts her head to one side and sticks her tongue out.

I love how she's always silly like that. "Really? That's hard for me to believe." I swat Josie Lee on the shoulder.

She shakes her head and flicks her hair back dramatically. "Yeah, I know it's hard to believe...someone as great as me."

We both laugh at the same time.

"There are not a lot of girls out there who actually *get* me. I know I can be a little *much* at times." Josie Lee rolls her eyes. "At least, that's what my dad says." She pauses for a moment, then smiles at me. "But, I think I may have found one who does."

I smile back. "Yeah. I think we make a really great pair."

"See. I told you we were soul sisters. It's like we just get each other. It's effortless with you." She flips her hair to the other side.

Josie Lee's eyes open wide. "You want to seal the deal? I have a great idea."

I bite at my cuticle. "Seal *what* deal?"

"Our bond, our friendship. So it's never broken. We'll always be connected." She swats my hand out of my mouth.

Excited with the thought, I respond, "Ok, sounds cool. How, though?"

She shoves me off the bed, "To become blood sisters. Hurry up, and go get a sharp object!"

A little scared and hesitant, I respond, "What? What for? We're already connected for life."

"We already know we're soul connected, so let's be blood sisters too. We have to cut our thumbs and then shake on it." She shrugs her shoulders. "That's how you do it...I would assume."

Thinking about this crazy idea for a few seconds, I bolt out of my bedroom into my bathroom. "Ok, stay right here."

I take out a fake rose from inside a flower pot plant, grab it, and then run back to my bedroom. Afterward, I bounce back onto the bed and sit back in the same upright position, chucking it over to her. "Here."

It has a sharp point at the end of the stem that holds it into place with the Styrofoam from inside the pot. Josie Lee looks at the rose and studies it for a second. She brushes her thumb up against the blade. It slices a perfect slit in her skin, and she bleeds. "Pretty clever. Ok, now hurry, give me yours."

I give my hand to her, close my eyes, and clench my other hand into a fist.

"Loosen up. Stop being such a baby. It doesn't hurt that bad." My skin slices open as she runs the blade along my thumb.

I bleed and open my eyes to look. "Ouch! That hurt. It's making me queasy."

"I think it looks yummy. I always wanted to be a vampire."

24

Josie Lee looks at her bleeding thumb, and she shoves it close to my face. "Better to suck you with, my dear."

"Eww. You're insane in the brain." I squirm. "Let's get it over with already."

We mesh our two thumbs into one, and the blood smudges.

"Ok, it's done. We sealed the deal," Josie Lee confirms. "We're officially blood sisters for life."

With the other hand, I hold it up in the air, awaiting a slap. "Cool. We did it. High five?" My non-bleeding hand is waiting for a response from her.

"Sure, dork. High five." she says with a sarcastic tone, slapping my hand back.

"Oh, right. And I'm the dork?"

Again, we can't stop laughing.

I WAKE up in the middle of the night. My alarm clock reads 1:28 a.m. Josie Lee is next to me on my bed with her hair covering most of her face, and her mouth hangs slightly open. Soft mumbles roll out from under her breath in her dreamy state of sleep. The television is on in the background. We must have passed out at some point watching the movie *Practical Magic*. Being it's the month of October, all the Halloweeny-type stuff is on. Fall is our favorite time of the year. It's because the weather starts to break and cool, holidays start coming up, and all the fun church carnivals come into town.

I notice the creepy board-game lying on the floor, next to the side of the bed. Just thinking about our dead spirit contact the night before sends quivers up and down my spine.

I roll over and pull the covers up close to my face. As I start to fall back into a sleep, I hear something just outside my bedroom window. It sounds like a rattling around in the tree branches. About a minute or two goes by, and I don't hear anything anymore, so I try to fall back to sleep. But, then again, just as I'm dozing, I hear the same sound. Feeling annoyed, I huff and puff getting out of my bed because I have to see what's making all this ruckus. I walk over to my window and take a quick peek outside. There's a pretty oak tree that sits right outside our front yard, next to our mailbox. And I swear, I see a small figure staring back at me in the shadows. I rub my eyes and look back because I'm still in that foggy sleep-state. But, when I open them, I catch a glimpse of sparkling glitter swirl around in the air and *swoosh* by my window. I even hear a small gust of wind that follows it. *Holy Mackerel!* It freaks me out.

I shove my bedroom window open to try and get a better view. "Hello," I say out the window. "Who's there?" But, nothing. Whatever or whoever it was is now gone. I'm left with a familiar whiff of gardenias. *Is that my mom's gardenia bush?* It's too strong to be coming from there. *Where is that scent coming from?* I close the window and back up. *What was that?* Being I'm a little scared, and I don't want Josie Lee to notice, I don't even bother waking her up. She'll just make fun of me, calling me a wimp or something.

I crawl back under my covers, shaking. This time I take them all the way up and over my head. Due to the eerie time of year, the supernatural movies we've been watching, and that freaky board-game that talks to spirits we played, my mind must be trippin' out. At least, that's what I hope.

CHAPTER THREE

A Visit to the Psychic

IT SOUNDS like some sort of harp and flute are playing in the room. Chimes hang from the ceiling, and as the air conditioner clicks on, it rattles them together. The store is filled with books, candles, crystals, and even a fortune teller. It smells of incense burning. It has many treasures—statues of all sorts of cool, supernatural creatures, like fairies, dragons, and even unicorns. There are books on the here and afterlife, reincarnation, etc.

"Come and check this out." In my hand she places a little statue fairy with long, sandy-blonde hair and hazel eyes. The pointy ears poke out behind her hair, and she wears a light blue, glittery dress. She's gazing down to the right at her feet. Her arms hang slightly out, and she has green ivy wrapped around her ankles, arms, and wrists. Marvelous iridescent white-blue wings sprout out on both sides of her back, and a big, pearl necklace lies perfectly around her neck.

"She's my favorite one here," Josie Lee's eyes sparkle as she stares at the statue. "There's just something exceptional about her."

I nod. "Wow. This place *is* awesome," I say as my eyes pan the entire store.

"I told you that you would love it, didn't I?" Josie Lee pulls me by the arm.

At that moment, a beautiful, heavy-set woman walks out from behind two, red velvet curtains. She has short, black-red hair, deep blue eyes, and is drenched in silver jewelry. Her dark eye makeup makes her blue eyes pop, and dark, red lipstick highlights her pale skin. She smiles kindly while approaching us with a slight limp in her stride.

"Can I help you with anything, darlings?" The woman huffs with a heavy breath. As her fingers meet her face to wipe some sweat beads from her forehead, I can't help but notice her perfect, red long nails and can feel a warm energy.

"Umm, no thank you," Josie Lee smiles back. "We're just looking for now."

"Ok, well, just let me know if there is anything I can do." The heavy-set woman arranges some books neatly on one of the shelves. "I work here. I'm a psychic-medium, so if either of you are interested in a reading today, we're having a special—forty dollars for half an hour."

I look at Josie Lee wide-eyed. It's like looking in the mirror.

"Should we do it?" I ask, nudging Josie Lee, almost knocking her over. "I'd love to see what it's like—I never have before."

Josie Lee catches her balance. "You go. I've done it before. It's cool. Definitely worth it." Browsing around the store she picks up a purple stone and observes it.

"I only have twenty dollars on me, though," I say.

"I'll spot you the other twenty," Josie Lee puts the stone down. She digs through her purse and wallet. "I can't pass up the chance to see your face when she reads you your future." Big, blue eyes protrude from her face.

"Really? You will? Awesome! I'll pay you back later. Promise." While she takes her time taking the money out of her wallet, I do this excited jitter-dance.

"Don't worry about it, spaz-attack. I've got it covered. Treat me to lunch at the mall or something. No biggie," she says, handing the other twenty dollars to me.

At this point we are both jumping up and down.

"So, is that a 'yes', darlings? If so, I only have so much time before my next appointment." The woman looks at her watch. "Come back in here to my special quarters then." She motions for us to walk to the back of the store, behind the curtains.

Josie Lee and I look at each other and giggle.

"Yes, it's a 'yes'," I wiggle. "I'm so nervous."

We all walk through.

In the room is a round table with two, plastic chairs. There is a crystal ball and a deck of tarot cards on the table.

"Ok, darlings, who's going today?" The woman asks with one big breath.

Raising my hand, I say, "I am."

The psychic-medium sits down and points to the chair in front of me. "Sit here, darling." She then addresses Josie Lee. "You can sit on the floor next to her. Sorry, not much room in here. I don't usually have more than one customer at a time."

The psychic-medium begins to shuffle her tarot cards. She looks me in the eyes, then Josie Lee. A white candle and incense both burn. "I'm going to do something I never ever do, but I have a feeling about you two. I'm going to read both of you for one fee. You girls are unique. It's like you come together as a package deal or something."

I smile at the lady then at Josie Lee. "Cool. Thanks."

"Ok. What's your name, darling?" she asks looking at me.

Then, she looks over at Josie Lee on the floor. "And your friend's?"

"I'm Seraphina—" I point to myself, then at Josie Lee "—and that's Josie Lee."

Josie Lee, sitting Indian-style on the floor, flips all of her hair to one side and gives a slight, somewhat sarcastic wave to the lady.

"Well, it's nice to meet both of you. My name is Leena. I can read your cards and also tell you messages I receive from spirits on the other side—some you may even know that have passed on."

I drop my mouth slightly. Josie Lee's arms are resting and dangling over her knees, kind of unaffected. *How is it that my insides are racing with excitement, while she's sitting there all cool and collected?*

Leena hands me the deck of tarot cards. "Please, shuffle these cards. Take some deep breaths, and think about things going on in your life that you want to focus on. Then, cut the deck in three parts. When you're done, put them together in one pile, and then hand them back to me."

I do what Leena tells me. Leena picks up the cards from the table and lays them back down, one-by-one, in different patterns.

Leena takes a few moments to examine the cards. Her voice is soft and sweet, and her breath is still heavy. "I see that you have recently moved. Is that correct?"

"Goodness gracious! Yes. How did you know that?"

Leena continues the reading, not paying much attention to my excitement. "It seems as if you are unsure about your surroundings and somewhat scared. However, someone is changing that for you. There is a person that is coming into your life who is going to be very influential—someone you are going to be extremely close with."

Waiting for the next sentence to spill out, I glower at Leena.

Leena continues, "This person will change you forever...change your destiny. Do you understand?"

I nod, not knowing what else to do.

Josie Lee sits up—more alert now—with her legs up and her arms still resting on her knees, all of her hair still to one side. Now, I can tell that Leena really has Josie Lee's attention.

"Who? Who is this person?" I shift in my chair.

"Your soulmate." Leena responds simply.

Josie Lee interjects. "No way! Not fair."

Leena looks at Josie Lee and then at me, "But not like the one you think. It's more of a...a *friend*. There's a big misconception in our society on soulmates. They don't necessarily have to be the opposite sex or in a romantic way. And we all can have more than one soulmate. It's just that rare, electric chemistry between two individuals. You know it when you meet them. Trust me."

"But—but who is this person?" My heart races. I turn to face Josie Lee in shock, and Leena follows my gaze.

"Exactly." Leena points to Josie Lee. "It's her. She's your soulmate—more like a soul sister." Leena reexamines the tarot cards lying out in front of her. "I knew I felt something electrifying between you two. You know? It's rare to find. You're both blessed."

Both our jaws drop, while Josie Lee's eyes are bugging from her head.

A few seconds pass.

"The message that I'm receiving is that you two are not blood-related sisters, but you are sisters connected by the soul."

"Well, actually we kind of are now." Josie Lee snorts.

"You're eternally connected through time and space. It can be nerve-wrenching for soulmates here at the same time living together on planet Earth, because it can be very risky." She's looking at one tarot card now in particular, with two hearts intertwined by some sort of ribbon.

I turn to face Leena again. "Wh-what do you mean? How?"

"Because you're both too connected for this fragile, emotional planet; and if something bad happens to one of you, it will be very hard for the other to bear. It will be like a piece of you is gone forever," she says addressing me. "The soulmate relationship can be one of the toughest. They're meant for our spiritual growth." Leena seems to be examining my face for expressions; her hands are now interlaced in almost a prayer-like fashion.

Josie Lee throws her arms up in the air. "Oh goodness! I knew it. I knew we knew each other in a previous life. I've said it before." She shakes her head.

Looking at Josie Lee in a grim manner, "Yes, darling." Leena replies. "You two know each other in every life. But, usually while one lives, the other is something of a spiritual guide to the other." Leena pauses. She analyzes both of us – pondering while rubbing the bottom of her chin. "However, I'm not sure why your souls chose to come here at the same time *this* time around. Hmm?"

I feel it must be simpler than that—maybe we just want to hang around each other. "Maybe we'd just miss each other too much." I place my hands over my heart, smiling at Josie Lee.

She makes one of her ridiculous, funny faces back at me; flaring her nostrils and making a gurgling sound with the back of her throat. She looks ridiculous doing it, but I can't help but love it on some weird level.

"This may not be a thing to cheer about, darlings. Yes, you girls of course are extremely bonded and will always miss the other when not around, but, no, that's not the reason you both chose to come here together." She shakes her head.

Josie Lee becomes irritated, using both hands to make the quotation gesture. "Well, what is 'the reason' then?"

"Something really significant is going to happen that is going to help you both save the world." Leena pauses and stops as if she's almost trying to hear or receive a message from the Spirit world. "However, Spirit isn't showing me what that is."

Josie Lee leaps up.

"Hokey-dokey, then." Josie Lee shouts sarcastically. She pulls at my arm. "I mean, really?" Josie Lee says to Leena. "I usually even believe in this stuff. But this is just ridiculous. Save the world?' Come on, let's go, Seraphina." Josie Lee continues to pull at my arm even harder.

I stand up. "Yeah, I mean, how are two young kids like us going to know how to 'save the world?'" I bite at my cuticle.

"I'm just channeling the messages I receive—I'm not the creator of your destiny." Leena wipes some sweat from her upper lip and chokes out a couple loud breaths. "If you give me one more minute, let me just concentrate some more, and see if anything else comes to me." Her eyes shut, and she takes a long inhalation.

Josie Lee looks at me and rolls her eyes. A few seconds pass.

Then, Leena opens her eyes and flips over another card of a golden star shooting across a sky. "Yes, yes. Ok, I got it." Leena gazes at us. "The two of you were supposed to meet on earth and wish on a shooting star together that you will both see. That's very important. Making this wish will be essential for your future and alter your lives and the lives of those on our planet forever."

At that moment, the light in the room flickers on and off, and then, it just stops.

Leena looks at this antique lamp sitting next to her on the table. She jiggles the bulb a bit, which seems to be fine now.

"No, it's not the bulb. That must be Spirit confirming what I'm saying."

With her arms crossed in front of her chest, posture upright and uptight, Josie Lee is gawping at Leena. I can't help but wonder what she is thinking, but by the look of her body language, it's pretty obvious. The vibes are strong.

"Ok. Now it's really time to go," Josie Lee says to me. "Give her the money. Let's get out of here already; I'm starting to get an anxiety attack." Josie Lee fans her hand in front of her face.

I grab my wallet, take the money out, and hand it to Leena. "Ok, thank you, that will be all for today."

"Yeah. Thanks for freaking us out," Josie Lee whispers under her breath.

Leena reaches out to take the money, "Thank you, and I'm sorry if this has upset both of you. But I'm meant to tell you both that as long as you see this shooting star together, you both pick the same, deepest desire of your hearts, and believe in its magic, that the wish will come true."

"Look." Josie Lee is now waving her hands around in the air in a dramatic way. "This sounds great and all, but we just really wanted to hear something like...you'll meet a cute, rich boy one day who you'll marry, have a white-picket fence and four children—two boys and two girls—and live happily ever after."

"Well, something along those lines, yeah." I shoot a dirty look at Josie Lee, then the fiddling with a loose piece of skin on my thumb begins. Always helps the nervousness.

Josie Lee yanks on my arm once again to leave. We turn to walk out of the room.

"Well, that's just the message I'm getting from Spirit, and I always tell my customers what Spirit says to me. I'm sorry if it got you both so upset. But the fact is that you two girls are special and have been called to a very important mission in this lifetime." Leena picks up the tarot cards. "It's your souls' contracts—there is no getting by it. It's how you choose, though, which will determine what path you both end up on. So, choose wisely. I know you don't believe me now, but you will. In time, you'll see."

Josie Lee stops and turns to face Leena, walking closer to her. "Thank you, but that's enough for today," she tells her. "We're leaving now. Bye," she says stomping away.

Following her, we leave from behind the red velvet curtains.

CHAPTER FOUR

A Pact

PARKED outside the store in the front as we leave is a black SUV. My mom waves her hand. "Girls. Girls, I'm right here."

Josie Lee and I are gripping onto each other for dear life, tittering as we walk over to the vehicle. It's hard to wrap my brain around what just took place with the psychic, and I can sense that Josie Lee feels the same way I do being she's clinging onto my body.

I climb into the front seat of my mom's car, while Josie Lee hops into the backseat.

"So, how was it?" My mom turns her whole body to look behind her as she reverses the car out of the parking lot.

We giggle at the same time. I turn around in my seat and examine Josie Lee's face. "Let's just say that it was really freaky."

Josie Lee's arms are folded by her chest. "Yup. You can say that again."

My mom glances at me, then at Josie Lee in the rearview mirror. "Why do you girls say that?"

I turn to face the window. "Never mind, Mom. You wouldn't get it."

"Wow, honey. Didn't know you gave me such little credit in life," my mom responds, looking at the road ahead. "You know, I've been through some things and seen a lot. Try me, I might understand."

I whip around, facing Josie Lee. "Go ahead, why don't you tell her how it went?"

Josie Lee scoots forward, pulling her body up closer to both of us in the front. She wraps her hands around the back of my head rest, looking at my mom. "Well,would you believe us if we told you that the psychic said that we were soulmates meant to live in this lifetime together because we would eventually 'save the world?'"

At that moment, my mom gets a red light; she slams on her brakes, and the car comes to a quick stop, making a loud screeching noise.

My mom scrunches up her face. "Sorry, girls. What was that again? Why would she say such a crazy thing and put that in your young minds?"

"That's exactly what we said." I glance out the window, watching the outside world in almost a different light now. Clouds accumulate in the sky, the birds are chirping on the power lines, and two squirrels are chasing each other up a tree. *Save the world in this big world? My heart races with the thought. No way.*

My mom puts her hand over her heart in exasperation. "Oh, good. So, you didn't believe that crazy lady? What some people will say or do to make a quick dollar. I mean, I should turn my car around and go back there and tell her…"

"Mom!" I shout. "See I told you. Don't you dare. You will

embarrass me." I put my head down and place my hand on my forehead.

Still at the red light, my mom looks over at me, then tucks a loose strand of my hair behind my ear. "Ok, honey. I won't. I'm just upset because I think that it is irresponsible for a grown adult to put those thoughts..."

I hit my mom's hand away. "Mom, please. We know. We don't believe her. It was just for fun." I look back at Josie Lee again, and our eyes lock. It's almost as if we're reading each other's thoughts.

"Ok. Promise. I won't." My mom continues driving, making a turn at the light. "Ok, well, just don't go visiting that crazy lady again, ok?"

"*Ok*, we won't, Mom." I roll my eyes.

"Anyway, where am I dropping you two off at? Or do you want to come grocery shopping with me?"

I put my hands around my throat pretending to choke myself. "Good grief. Spare us, please. Grocery shopping?"

Josie Lee chuckles at my drama act. "Actually, I wanted to know if you could drop us off at my house? I wanted Seraphina to sleep over tonight. Is that ok?" she asks my mom, smiling and holding onto the back of my head rest.

"I don't know, sweetheart. You girls are spending an awful lot of time together," my mom responds. "It might be good to take a little break from each other—give each other some space."

Simultaneously, we both shake our heads and say aloud, "Nah." I love that she always finishes my thoughts. *So in sync.*

My mom glances at me and then back at Josie Lee while still driving. "I mean, I don't know how your parents feel about it. I haven't spoken with your mom."

I tug on my mom's arm. "Oh, please, Mom, please."

"Seraphina, stop it!" my mom shouts back. "You're going make us crash."

My mom lets out a big *sigh* then pauses for a brief moment. "I guess I have no problem with it. As long as your mom doesn't mind, Josie Lee."

Josie Lee flips her hair to the side. "Please. My mom? She couldn't care less. Only thing she cares about is *my dad*. Ekkk." She pinches my cheek. "Plus, who would mind this face of a movie star?"

I scrunch up my nose at her; she then follows back with another funny face, tilting her head to one side, crossing her eyes, and sticking out her tongue.

My mom veers off the far-right lane, and switches on her turn signal. She turns around checking her blind spot. "Alright then. I guess it's off to your house, Josie Lee."

I clap my hands. "Yay! Thanks, Mom."

I start changing all the radio stations to settle on a song that I like. I'm about to change it again, when Josie Lee begins jumping up and down in her seat, then she smacks me on the arm. "Ooh. Ooh. I love this song. Don't' change it—turn it up."

Rubbing the place on my arm where Josie Lee smacked it, I proceed to turn the song up loud.

She flips her hair around wild, singing and knowing all the words, "So baby pull me closer in the backseat of your Rover..."

Whipping around in my seat to get a good glance at her, I can't help but laugh. "You're completely nuts."

Josie Lee breaks for a second to respond, smiling. "Admit it. You love it." She then opens her mouth and makes this nasally gurgling sound with the back of her throat. There's even a glimpse of Josie Lee's tonsils, her mouth is so wide open.

I can't explain her quirkiness. You just have to see it to understand. But, I just get her. Laughing so hard at this moment, I hold my stomach. "Ok, I love it." I lean my head against the head rest, grinning. I can't help but sing with her. "We ain't ever getting older."

"You two are so silly." My mom shakes her head.

~

JOSIE LEE SWINGS open the front door of her light-pink, one-story home. When we walk in, I can smell the aroma of tuna and cheese baking in the oven.

Josie Lee's mom is preparing dinner—making and dressing a tossed house salad, while she waits for the tuna casserole to finish. Her brown, mixed with grey, curly hair is held back by a purple scrunchy. *Wow. Don't see those often anymore.* As she leans down to open the oven to check out the casserole, her glasses slide down to the tip of her nose, almost falling off. She catches them before they hit the floor next to her white and purple slippers. Wearing a silk, flowered nightgown, it looks like she's from some other era.

Josie Lee and I pass by the kitchen to walk to the sliding glass door.

"Yum. Smells really good, Mom!" Josie Lee yells while passing her dad, who is lying in his recliner. We walk through the sliding glass doors to the patio.

His crystal blue eyes never sway from watching golf on television; apparently his everyday routine from what Josie Lee has told me. Josie Lee has his same eyes.

I can't help but notice his white skin, which blends in with the colors red, white, and blue. He has on a baseball hat, coach shorts, and his socks are pulled up all the way to his knees. *Hmm? Weird. Must be very patriotic, or something.*

"Hey, Dad."

However, her dad doesn't acknowledge Josie Lee or me. Before we slip outside completely, her mom calls out from the kitchen. "Dinner will be ready in about a half hour. I expect both of you to be in here to eat. I'm making your favorite...tuna casserole, extra cheesy. Just how you like it."

"Fine. Can you just bring us out some sweet tea?" Josie Lee snaps. "Nice outfit, Mom," she mumbles under her breath.

We sit down on the wood, patio-swing set with a green canopy. Josie Lee sits on one side and I on the other; we swing back and forth. After a few minutes of conversation and giggles, the clouds start to turn grey and rumble. Sweat beads tickle the sides of my temples a little, but I don't mind. And from Josie Lee going on and on about this and that, waving her hands in the air as she speaks about how annoying it is that her dad wears red, white, and blue every day of his life, and how her mom is so nerdy, she doesn't seem to be too bothered either.

Her mom walks outside to hand us two, cold glasses of sweet tea. "Dinner will be ready soon, ok?"

Nobody responds. I look at Josie Lee's mom. She is looking at Josie Lee, and Josie Lee is looking at me.

"Josie Lee...ok?" Her mom sounds agitated.

Even though Josie Lee has her dad's eyes, she has her mom's face. Long with a pointed chin, and they both have that same mole above their heart-shaped lips. Except Josie Lee is always smiling with these big, white teeth. I've only seen her mom smile once so far, and they both have that little gap between their two front teeth.

"Ok, Mom! I heard you the first time. For Pete's sake!"

Ignoring Josie Lee, her mom turns around to walk back into the house.

Little rain drops, that peek out from underneath the canopy-top, scatter on our arms a bit.

"I was thinking that after dinner and our movie, we can sneak out and go over to the clubhouse pool—stare up at the stars. It's so much fun. I do it all the time and my parents never catch me." Josie Lee happily continues her interrupted conversation with me.

"I don't know, Josie Lee." I hesitate. "I'm fine with just me and you hanging out here all night. You know? Inside where it's safe and we don't get into any trouble."

"It's no big deal. Come on. Don't be such a scaredy-cat."

"Of course it is. I don't want to get caught." I take a sip of her mom's homemade sweet tea, which is delicious. My lips smack from the perfect combination of sweetness and lemon.

"We won't. I know how to do it perfectly now. You'll see. Trust me," she says with a big grin on her face.

"I guess." I shrug my shoulders.

Josie Lee sticks her tongue out at me.

Smiling sarcastically at her, I become distracted from what I see behind her head. I point. "Holy Mackerel! Look at that beautiful rainbow."

Josie Lee turns around and gawks at it for a few seconds. "Wow. That's the prettiest rainbow I think I've ever seen."

The rainbow covers the whole entire sky with all its vibrant colors.

"How does that happen?" I ask.

Josie Lee is still turned around staring. "I think it's like the perfect combination of water and light, or something like that. You'll learn soon. I was just taught that in school this past year. It's really just a miracle."

"I always imagined a world inside there, or at least maybe that's where we go when we die." I say in amazement.

Josie Lee turns back around to face me, looking somewhat surprised. "What do you mean?"

I take another sip of my sweet tea. "I mean that maybe like when we die, we just go inside a rainbow. Or maybe heaven just looks like what a world would look like inside a rainbow or something like that."

Josie Lee chuckles, takes a sip of her sweet tea, then she kind of tilts her head to one side.

"I don't know what I mean, or what I'm trying to say," I feel a little stupid now and shake my head. "I'm confusing. Sorry."

"No. No. I think I get what you're trying to say," Josie Lee sits up-right in her chair and leans in closer. "It's pretty cool, actually. Tell me more." She gathers more speed for us on the patio swing.

I feel myself blush; I've never told anyone stuff like this before. "Well, you said a rainbow is a miracle, right? And aren't rainbows really just an illusion or something like that?"

She takes a sip of her sweet tea again and nods.

I start picking at my cuticle on my thumb. "Then maybe our heaven is a place that we just create for ourselves. Like, it's whatever we want it to be or look like. And I guess I would want mine to look like what I imagine it would be like inside a rainbow." Looking down at my now loose piece of skin, I don't gather up enough guts to glance back at Josie Lee. *What must she be thinking? This sounds crazy.*

"Oooh. Sounds awesome. I love where you're going with this. Keep it coming. So what would your heaven look like?"

Oh, she digs it. Cool. I now build up the nerve to look at her in the eyes.

Josie Lee is gleaming from ear to ear.

"Well, it would have all the colors like a rainbow. Like each realm will have its own color, you know?" I continue on. "And each world with its own mystical creatures—like those fairies and unicorns we saw earlier in Leena's store. And even sunflower fields that go on for miles."

Her pretty blues with those long eyelashes flicker and bulge from her face. "Quite the imagination. Didn't know you had it in ya'?"

"Yeah, well, I guess I do believe in some sort of an afterlife or other world out there," I say. "My mom always did tell me that I had a wild imagination. Maybe I'll be a great writer or storyteller someday." I say, grinning.

Josie Lee leans over the small wooden table in between us and throws me a slight love punch on my shoulder from the other side of the swing. Looking at me in a more serious manner, she busts out with, "If you're a believer, than so am I. You're my best friend, so we stick together. Plus, you're the only person in the world I really trust anyway."

We both smile.

"And let me tell ya' something," Josie Lee adds. "It would be pretty fresh if there really did exist a world inside a rainbow because I would go there in a heartbeat; escape this wacky house with my weird mom and zombie dad."

"Hey, why are you so hard on your mom? She isn't all that bad." I say.

She rolls her eyes. "Yeah, right. If I have to watch my mom slave over him for one more minute without an ounce of appreciation, I might vomit. I mean, how does she put up with him? His existence is useless. He just stares at that stupid TV all day, watching golf in the same stupid clothes. It's pathetic."

With my elbows resting on my knees, I lean in closer to her. "Just cut her some slack. She seems to really care about you, and at least she tries to show it."

She sighs with another roll of the eyes. "Whatever. Maybe if I did escape inside a different world and were gone, maybe then he'd realize I was alive in the first place."

"Ok, well, listen. Let's make a pact then, ok?" I reach out my hand for Josie Lee to shake. "If it exists, somehow, one day, we'll both meet up there and have the adventure of our lives. I wouldn't mind getting out of my own nuthouse for a bit myself."

Josie Lee cracks a smile and reaches out her hand to meet mine. They interlock.

She smirks and holds her index finger in the air. "Ok. But, only under one condition."

"And what's that?" I ask, sighing. This time I'm rolling *my* eyes.

"That this world has like witches, trolls, and some eerie stuff in it too."

"Are you serious?"

She nods her head.

"You are *so* weird! Why?" But then again, this *is* Josie Lee.

"I don't know. I love the unknown, that scary mysteriousness, I guess. Plus, I think it just gives it a twist. It makes it more interesting and exciting." She sticks her hands out and twitches her body from side to side.

I tap my temple with my forefinger. "You have some screws loose upstairs."

"I know." Josie Lee giggles.

"Great. My best friend is a nutcase."

We both laugh in sync.

"So, we're in agreement then? That if two seats open up, we're buying tickets?" I ask again for reassurance.

Josie Lee winks and makes a gun gesture with her hand and pretends to shoot. "You better believe it."

The sliding glass door opens at that moment, and Josie Lee's mom shouts over to us. "Ok, girls, dinner is ready. Come in and eat."

She rubs her belly. "Perfect, just in time. I'm starved. My favorite—cheesy tuna casserole." Josie Lee gets up from the swing, skips to the sliding glass door, and then hops inside. I follow behind her in a more modest way.

We sit at the oval-shaped dining room table and join her parents. In front of us, the tuna casserole steams. Her mom scoops up a big piece for her husband and drops it down on his plate. His eyes never leave golf on the television. Josie Lee shakes her head. Then her mom scoops some tuna casserole for Josie Lee and me. I'm the only one at the table who acknowledges her mom. "Thank you."

Josie Lee taps me on the arm. She starts playing with her food as she collects it on her fork. She opens her mouth wide and takes a large bite, chewing her food very slowly. After that, she picks up her glass of sweet tea and takes a big gulp with her eyes closed, indulging in the taste, following with a sigh of refreshment. "You have to take the perfect bite. You get the perfect combination of noodles, tuna, and cheese onto your fork. Then, you wash it down with a gulp of tea." Josie Lee pauses a brief second, looking at me. "Go on, do it."

I stare at her open-mouthed, trying to figure out where in the world she comes up with these goofy things, but I do it anyway. Making her happy is all I want to do, so I copy her actions. I gulp and sigh myself.

Josie Lee is watching my every move, smiling and nodding. "Good, right? See, I told you."

"Yes. It really is the perfect bite." I giggle.

"Can we watch a movie later in the living room?" she asks her mom.

"That shouldn't be a problem. As long as you girls keep the noise level down. You don't want to bother your dad." Looking at Josie Lee's dad for acknowledgment, her mom takes a bite of tuna casserole. He just continues to watch golf.

"Oh, no. We wouldn't want that now." Josie Lee rolls her eyes.

I nudge Josie Lee underneath the table and give her the nasty eye, but she doesn't even acknowledge me.

Smacking her lips, savoring her every bite, she says to her mom, "When we're done with the movie, we want to go over to the pool clubhouse to star-gaze."

I nudge her even harder under the table. Josie Lee just remains unaffected, examining her parents for reactions.

Her mom stays silent, chewing her food. After a few seconds, her eyes pan over to Josie Lee's dad who is also silent for a bit, chewing his food. He takes a sip of tea. "No. It's too late for you to be out after the movie ends. You both can stay in tonight." He finally gives his input, his eyes staying focused on the television screen, all while picking up the napkin from the table, patting his mouth ever-so-lightly with it.

That may be the first time I ever heard Josie Lee's dad speak. I gaze at him not even thinking about messing with what he just said. "That's fine with me, Mr. Ryan; we don't have to go out."

A pinkish-red shade starts to surface on Josie Lee's face who's now holding her breath. *Uh-oh.* I know that look. I hope that she doesn't push her luck. "Right, Josie Lee? Tell him. We don't have to go out."

Josie Lee doesn't take her eyes off of her dad. Feeling it coming, I cringe inside. She *slams* her fists on the table. "Dad! No, Dad! That's not fair! I want to go out, and we're going to out and do what we want!"

Oh, no she didn't. She went there. I can feel the heat building up inside my body. That little trickle of sweat even starts to form between my boobies.

A big chunk of uneaten tuna casserole still sits on her fork as she waves it around in the air. "Mom? Please... help me here... tell him something, please?"

Her mom doesn't look at Josie Lee, she is concentrating on eating—chewing her food so slowly that you think it's on purpose. *Maybe it is.*

"Josie Lee, you just have to do what your dad tells you."

A big puff of air gusts out of her mouth; she stands up from the table and pulls me by the arm, still examining her parents' detached response. "This isn't fair! You never let me do anything that I want!"

She yanks me by the arm. "Come on."

I'm just about to put another bite of food in my mouth, but the fork drops out of my other hand, which makes a loud *clank*. It hits the plate. "Josie Lee. I'm not finished with my dinner."

However, I know I don't stand a chance against Josie Lee's strong will and stubbornness. So, I surrender and follow her into her bedroom.

She slams the bedroom door shut behind us, falling onto her bed crying.

I stroke her back. "Josie Lee, it's ok. Come on. It's not that big a deal. We'll do it another night."

Josie Lee lifts her face from her hands, and props her head up to look at me. Her face is wet with tears. "No. We're just going to have to still sneak out."

I raise my hands in the air. "I know, hello? I thought that was the original plan? Why did you even say anything? I can't sneak out now. If we get caught, I'll be grounded for the rest of my life."

"Good. Then I'll just sleep over your house for the rest of mine," she mumbles with her face back in her hands.

"Yeah, ok, sure. Whatever. Like your parents would ever let that happen."

"Whatever, like my dad even cares. He wouldn't notice if I disappeared off of the planet. Nobody cares about me. I should just vanish." Josie Lee lets out a big *sniffle*.

My heart sinks from the thought, and I give her a light slap on the back of her head. "Don't say that. I care about you, and your mom cares about you." *Really not sure about her dad. He's an odd-ball.* But, I wouldn't say that to her and make her feel worse.

Josie Lee *sniffles* in her hands.

"Why don't you cut her a break?" I ask. "I mean, you're the one who even said that watching your dad not appreciate her makes you want to vomit. Remember?"

As her sobs come to a stop, she lifts up her face again. "Yeah. I guess you're right." She wipes her tears away.

I delight in doing a little dance. "I know I'm right."

Cracking a smile and nudging me slightly, she then props herself up on the bed to face me. "Whatever, dork. Get over yourself."

"It made you smile, though, didn't it?" I pause. "You alright? Can I please go finish my *perfect* bites now?" I make the gesture with my hand playing with a pretend fork and food. "I was enjoying that dinner your mom made. Your favorite, by the way."

She lets out a huge *sigh* again. "Fine. But we're sneaking out after the movie is over."

I wave my arms in the air. "You're relentless. If it makes you happy... fine, whatever you want, especially if it'll shut you up."

Josie Lee jumps up and down and wraps her arms around my neck, choking me. I make a *gurgling* noise in the back of my throat. "Ok, get off me, you're choking me." I pry her arms from around my neck.

Mashing my face together with her hands, she kisses me repeatedly. "I love you. I love you. I love you."

I step off the bed". "Alright already. You're like a little toddler, having to get what you want." Before I walk out of her bedroom door, I turn back to her. "Just don't get me in trouble please."

We both leave the bedroom to go back to the dining room table. No one speaks a word throughout the rest of dinner. The sound of forks *click* on the plates as everyone finishes eating. I take my time, relishing in my perfect bites.

CHAPTER FIVE

To Wish on a Shooting Star: Deepest Hearts' Desire

"JUST CLIMB OUT, COME ON." Josie Lee demands, referring to my feet that are stuck between the electric, blue carpet of Josie Lee's floor, and the hedges that are aligned below the outside of her window.

"I can't—I'm stuck."

She laughs at me hysterically.

"Oh, yeah, real funny," I say not finding any humor with one leg, dangling halfway out the window to meet the ground. "Sorry, I'm not a *professional* like you are at this."

I finally make my way through with a tumble to the ground, rolling right through the hedges to the sidewalk of her house.

"Hurry up...come on." She grabs me, yanking my arm like usual. Stop making so much noise, you're going to wake up the annoying people," she says, referring to her parents. "Let's go over to the clubhouse pool."

"I'm really not sure about this," I say.

"Oh, don't be such a baby." Her blue eyes peek out underneath a black head-band, holding her long bangs back as her blonde hair drapes over her shoulders in a natural, wavy way.

Twisting her body around to walk over to the clubhouse, I stumble behind her. I can't help but notice her coordinated outfit—black, tapered jeans, a tight, dark-purple tee, and black and white sneakers. She sways her body from side to side as she walks.

When we arrive, there's a big sign that reads No Entry Past 7 p.m. All Trespassers Will Be Fined. In my mind, that's called a rule.

Josie Lee plays with the gate latch to the clubhouse, and glides right through the gate with not a care in the world. She doesn't even peek around to make sure that there are no adults.

I pick at my cuticles. "I don't know about this." My hands end up in the pockets of my cut-off, jean shorts, and I kick around a pebble on the ground with silver, strappy, flat sandals.

Josie Lee is preoccupied with finding lounge chairs that we can lay on to gaze up at the stars. There's a rattling sound coming from the hedges a short distance away. I whip my body in that direction to look, and I swear I see that same small figure, staring at me again. My eyes squint to get a better look. A small poof of glitter is all that now remains in the air. "What?"

With a serious glare, she asks, "Why do you look like you just saw a ghost?"

"Did you see that?" I point in the direction of where I saw that small mystery.

"See what?" She thrashes around, looking in the direction where I'm pointing. "No. I don't see anything, Seraphina. What's wrong with you? You're just paranoid about getting caught. We're fine. My parents are deep sleepers. They would sleep through a burglary."

I try and think about something else, because I'm beginning to freak myself out. "Kind of hard for me to believe with them having a daughter like you." I pull my thick hair back into a ponytail because I can't handle the muggy humidity and sweat that's starting to form on the back of my neck. Just the thought of getting caught, and the weird figure I keep seeing, makes my heart beat faster. Waving my hand in my face, I try and fan myself.

She laughs at me and gives me a love-tap on my arm. "Don't be nervous. We'll be fine." We walk to the lounge chairs, sit, and stare up at the stars.

A few minutes pass. I forget about everything briefly, staring up at the stars in a somewhat meditative state. "You know what I'm thinking right now, don't you?"

Smiling, she turns to look at me, then back at the stars. "I think I can read your mind."

My arms fold up underneath my head, gazing up at the galaxy. "I mean, do you think it's even possible? Do you think she was telling the truth?"

"Who knows? I guess time will tell. I believe in destiny, so if it's meant to be, it will happen. But, there sure are a lot of crazy people out there." Josie Lee squirms in her chair.

I giggle. "Uh, yeah. You being one of them."

She throws me a light punch to the arm. "Shut up."

"Ouch! Can you stop hitting me all the time, please?" I rub my arm where it throbs a little. "I know. Come on. Us? 'Save the world'? Really?"

Just at that moment, a huge, bright star shoots across the sky. It's a flash so bright, it lights an illuminating trail of golden glitter, glistening until it slowly fades away. Both of us whisk our heads to face each other, and our mouths fly open. We both perk up at the same time.

"Cheese and peas!" Josie Lee shouts out. "Holy Mackerel! What was that? Did you just see what I saw?"

"Yes, I did. What was that?" Goosebumps raise hairs all over my body. "And isn't it, 'rice and peas?'"

"Yeah, but everything is better with cheese..." she replies a little calmer for a second, almost forgetting what we just saw. "That's not the point. I'm freaking out. What do we do now? Do we make a wish? This has to mean something huge." Her arms wave around in the air.

"Looked just like a shooting star to me." I jump to my feet.

"Well, what do we wish for? Did she say?" Josie Lee sits up even taller on the lounge chair.

"She said something like, 'the deepest desires of our hearts.'" Feeling the need to calm my nerves, I gaze once again at my cuticles, trying to find which piece of skin would be the best part to bite off.

"Right now? Well, that's easy for me. To disappear." Josie Lee bends her head back and waves it from side to side.

I can't help but squint my eyes at Josie Lee. "Are you kidding me? No, dodo-brain. We have to have the 'same' wish. I don't want to just disappear. That's no fun." I settle on the tiny piece of skin on my right index finger.

Putting her head back up straight, she holds her fingers to her mouth, wearing a disappointed expression on her face. "Oh, yeah. Crap, you're right. Then what? Any ideas?"

My head hangs down, thinking for a few seconds, and then I swing it up high. "I got it."

She now jumps up off her chair. "What? What? What is it?" She's doing the ants-in-her-pants dance.

"Alright. For Pete's sake...Give me a second to say it, will ya'?" I put my hand up in her face.

"Sorry. I just feel like it won't work if we wait too long."

"Ok, ok." I interrupt her. "You're making me nervous.

Remember when we said that if there was a world inside a rainbow, we would both go?"

"Yes. But what does that have to do with…" Josie Lee suddenly switches thoughts. "That's just too ridiculous. Is that even possible?"

"Well, I think 'ridiculous' became 'ridiculous' when she told us our fortune that day. And, this can't just be a coincidence. I mean, it's the only thing that I can think of that we both want. It sounds pretty cool, right? So, what can it hurt? Let's try it." My thoughts are racing with me. I place my hands on my hips, thinking it's got to be the best idea yet.

"Ok. Let's do it. You go first, though, it's your idea." She points to me.

Shutting my eyes and focusing, I say aloud, "Ok. I wish that if there is a world inside of a rainbow then me and my best friend, Josie Lee, can go there together."

Josie Lee copies my words and facial expression, yet she says it with her hands on her hips, and kind of jiggling her body around. "I wish that if there is a world inside of a rainbow then me and my best friend, Seraphina, can go there together."

Flashing light and an intense, loud rumbling sound blasts through the whole black, starry sky. We are both speechless for a few moments as this goes on. My heart is beating a thousand miles a minute as if I just ran down the street being chased. This can't be real. The floor underneath us begins shaking, where we both have to hold out our arms to brace ourselves. It's like an earthquake effect. However, we're in Florida, where there are no earthquakes. Then, it just ends.

"Good heavens! What just happened? I am totally freaked out right now." Josie Lee places her folded, shaking hands over her heart.

I'm still speechless.

"Seraphina? Earth to Seraphina!"

With very slow words, I say one-by-one, trying to get them out. "Guessing? I'd say our wish has just been answered."

"Yeah? Well, it's not exactly like we're inside a rainbow right now." Josie Lee pans her arms in front of us at the realistic view of a clubhouse and pool.

CHAPTER SIX

The Accident

I YAWN, wrapping up these last math equations before bed. *Homework really sucks.* It's Sunday night, and I have to turn it in tomorrow.

Instead, my mind drifts to shopping at the mall, going to the beach, or even going to all of the local church carnivals with Josie Lee. We've been inseparable.

It's now the twenty-eighth of January. Fall came and went, I turned ten in September, and Josie Lee turned eleven on December twenty-ninth, over winter break. *It all finished in a flash.* I had a low-key celebration with dinner, a movie, and a sleepover with just Josie Lee. My mom took us. Of course, Josie Lee went all out, inviting a bunch of friends over for a pool party at the clubhouse. At least the hot, humid weather is temporarily gone. It's now cool and in the low 70's most of the time. Sometimes the temperature drops even lower a bit. Florida is so nice in the winter.

I can't help but envision all of my old friends from New

Jersey, bundling up by fireplaces, getting snowed in from the crazy winter blast that has to have them freezing to death. *That, I don't miss. All that snow. The hassle that comes along with it... plowing, shoveling, bundling with scarves, hats, mittens, etc. Not too bad here after all.*

I peer up from my notepad and math equations for a moment, lost in thought, beaming with delight in the thought of my new life. It's all because of my best friend—my favorite person in the world right now—my soul sister, Josie Lee. Just to think when I first moved here, I never thought I'd ever make friends. But, she helped change that for me.

My parents are in the other room, watching television. It's fairly quiet besides the TV in the background. My dad loves to watch old Turner black and white classics. The telephone rings. I look at the clock on the kitchen stove, which reads 8:28. My mom gets up off the couch to answer it. "Hello?"

"Ok, ok, Penny, try and calm down. I can't understand you. Please."

I jump to my feet, and I leap over to my mom. A few seconds pass by. It's Josie Lee's mom on the other end. "What? Mom, what? What's wrong?" I tug her arm.

My mom puts her hand over her mouth. "Oh my goodness!"

My dad then gets off of the couch and walks over to us. "Honey? What is it? Is something wrong with Josie Lee's dad?" He assumes.

Tears begin to collect in my mom's eyes. "No. Oh no. Penny, I'm so sorry." She pauses. "Please, please let me know if there's anything I can do."

Now, I'm tugging at my mom's arm even harder. I can't hold off another minute; I feel like I may burst.

"Ok. So sorry. Bye." My mom hangs up the phone. She looks at my dad, frowning. She bites her lower lip, which trembles while she holds back the tears. "Oh no." Those words barely make it out of her mouth.

I'm staring at my mom with fear. My insides are on fire. *What can it be?* My dad has to be right. Something bad must have happened to Josie Lee's dad. *A heart attack or something?* Yeah, has to be. He is a lot older than Josie Lee's mom, by about fifteen years or something like that.

"Honey, it's Josie Lee," my mom says. Again, her lips tremble. This time even more.

I begin feeling panicky. My heart beats faster and faster with anticipation. I think it's now out of my chest in the back of my throat. "What? What happened?"

"There's been an accident."

"What do you mean, Mom? What happened?" Now, I can feel my lower lip starting to tremble as well.

My mom places her hands to her forehead. "She got into a fight with her dad and stormed out of the house." She pauses for a second.

I'm way too anxious to wait, so I snatch hold of my mom's elbow, removing her hand away from her face. "And?"

"Honey, I'm so sorry to say this..." again she pauses and can't hold back tears from rolling down her cheeks. "She was walking on the side of the road, and they didn't see her. A car hit her. They don't know if she's going to make it, honey. She's in a coma at the hospital."

I drop to my knees and look up at the ceiling with my hands in a prayer motion, bawling with every single ounce of my soul. *How can that be?* I just saw her. We were just sharing cheese crackers together at her house not too long ago. *This can't be happening. No! No!* I want somebody to shake me, wake me up, and tell me that this is all just some bad nightmare. *Pinch me hard.*

I can barely make the words out loud. "No...no...mommy... no!" I can't stop the crying or my hands shaking.

My heart feels like it has been ripped out of my chest and thrown against the wall, slowly sliding down.

My mom tries to wipe away my tears, but it's useless. She bends down to pick me up from the floor by wrapping her arms around me, but I just push her away.

Now, my dad steps in and heaves me up off the floor, walking off with me in his arms and carrying me into my bedroom.

From a short distance behind me, I can hear my mom's voice whisper these short words again, "Honey, I'm *so* very sorry." However, it sounds like an eternity.

AGAIN. A hard tug on my arm. My trance is pulled back to this dreadful hospital room. "Seraphina, Seraphina." We have to go now. It's time, honey. I'm sorry. You have to say your final goodbyes."

I whisk my body back around to realize she's gone. No more girl. No more Josie Lee with a shimmering gown. And that fairy boy? Gone now too. Even the flowery-smell is starting to fade away.

I see Josie Lee's mom, signing papers. She's sobbing hard. Her dad gets up and walks out of the room. He says nothing. No emotion; no tears. One nurse (not the same one who handed me the letter) is taking the tube out of her mouth. The doctor enters the room. He seizes the clipboard from Josie Lee's mom's trembling hands. She's holding onto it for dear life. She finally lets go. He walks over to the machines, and one by one, begins switching them off. The sound of them? Gone now too. It's quiet.

Everything in my body goes numb.

I hear my mom's voice again like a faint echo. "Come on, honey." She puts her arms around me, and supports me out of the room. I don't even know how I'm walking. Something else is guiding me—something much bigger than myself.

My mind must've been playing tricks on me. I was dreaming, hallucinating, or something. What I saw couldn't have really happened. If it was real, she wouldn't have disappeared; she wouldn't have left me. *Not Josie Lee. Not my soul sister.*

CHAPTER SEVEN

The Chosen One

I FEEL the need to walk, get some fresh air, and think about things, so I decide not to take the school bus home on this particular day. My heart aches to have Josie Lee back, and living without her doesn't seem fair. *How could this happen? How could God take away the only real friend I've ever had? Did I do something bad, something wrong? Was I being punished?* Josie Lee was too young to die.

I walk the street with my head held low. My back is hunched over as I kick at the dirt and street debris along the way. I can feel my hair frizzing up from drizzling rain. I wipe off the sweat from around my upper lip as tears flow down my cheeks. The sound of my sniffles seems to play a tune with the cars that are swarming by. Even some birds are forming a frantic chirping song because they know a late afternoon rainstorm is approaching.

Cutting through a little forest up ahead, that separates the walk between school and my neighborhood, I take a short-cut home as the sky begins to turn dark grey from the dreary, winter clouds, which are forming. This way I can take shelter with the trees to avoid getting too wet.

Usually it's nice here in winter, but on this particular day, there feels and looks like a peculiar aura in the air.

It begins to rain harder. Just as I'm about to enter the forest, I see a large, beautiful rainbow appear out of the corner of my eye.

There's a path that leads inside the forest; oak trees are everywhere. I take one last glimpse of the colorful rainbow, from what seems like a short distance away, and enter. My clothes are starting to cling a little bit to my body and my knees are wobbly.

I bellow out a sigh while taking a rest on a big, tree stump that sticks out from the ground. Slumping over my knees with the weight of my body, I throw my tote bag on the ground in exhaustion, put my head in my hands, and begin to sob. My sobbing gets louder and louder. Snot drips a little stream down into my mouth. I clench one fist, while the other hand hovers over my broken heart.

"Why, God?" I say aloud. "Why did she have to die? Can someone please explain to me why this happened?"

"Life always has a plan, you know?" says a squeaky voice. I jolt my head up, looking around, until my eyes become focused on this beautiful, multi-colored, talking butterfly perched on my knee. This butterfly has every shade of the rainbow throughout its small wings.

There's no way in this world that a butterfly can be speaking to me. "Who's there?" My head pans the surrounding forest area around me. There has to be a person hiding in the woods, behind a tree or something.

"Here. I'm right here." The little butterfly confirms, fluttering its wings.

Staring down at my knee for a moment, I take notice of this unique butterfly. I can't believe my eyes or ears. "What?"

The butterfly stays perched on my knee, but flutters his wings. "Don't be startled, please."

I jerk up to a standing position, and watch it casually fly off of my knee and land on my nose. My eyes cross to try and make out a tiny mouth moving on a tiny face. "Holy Mackerel!" I shake my head.

He continues to flutter his wings. "Nope. You're not seeing things. I'm really here."

"This can't be possible." Swatting at the butterfly, so he moves off of my nose, I have to take a step back to get a better look. "Am I really seeing what I think I'm seeing? Or am I so upset right now that I'm just delirious?" I close my eyes, rub them with my fists, and then reopen them to see if I can still make out this little butterfly's image. *Why do these crazy things keep happening to me lately?*

The butterfly sighs. Little words trickle out of his mouth. "No. You are *really* seeing what you're seeing."

He flies around my body. Iridescent shades of red, pink, orange, yellow, blue, violet, and even colors that I have never seen before vibrate a brilliant trail around me.

"But, how? Who? How is it possible that you are talking to me right now? Where did you come from?" I scramble for the right words.

The butterfly continues to flap around my face. "Listen. I know it's hard to believe, but *I am* real. My name is Sebastian. I exist inside a world of a rainbow called Raiven. You know? Just like the one you and your friend wished for."

My jaw drops, and I begin slapping myself in the head. I had completely forgotten about that wish...until now. "Um, ok, think. Did I fall and hit my head recently? Did my mom slip something in my tea last night? I mean, you have been under a lot of stress lately since Josie Lee died. Maybe..." I mumble to myself as if no one is there.

"Seraphina, no," Sebastian interrupts. "It's not any of those things. Please stop beating yourself up and listen."

I stop and look at him, stuttering. "How d-did you k-know my name?"

He *swooshes* by my nose around my head. "I know because you are the girl who made the wish to enter inside our world—you and Josie Lee did. We've been waiting on that person for a very long time. Didn't you receive the letter? From one of our messengers?"

It finally begins to sink in that I'm really having a conversation with a butterfly. This isn't some crazy dream. I drop back down onto the tree stump, putting my head in the palm of my hand as my arm rests on my leg. *How could I forget...the wish...that letter from the mysterious nurse? Yes, of course.*

"A messenger, huh?" I ask. "She didn't strike me as a real nurse."

Sebastian perches himself on my other knee, "I know this is all very hard for you, but I was sent to come get you, and we're running out of time. We have to go. It's urgent."

"Go where? I can't go anywhere with you. I'm already going to be in trouble because I'm coming home so late. *And wet.* If I don't come home, they'll call the troops to come out to find me. You don't know my family; they'll worry sick." Here goes the crying again.

The spastic butterfly bats his wings at lightning speed. His colors make a swirling wave in mid-air. "No, no, no. Please don't cry. I can't handle crying."

"What do you want from me then?" I prop my head back up and look at Sebastian getting all bent out of shape, so I contain myself.

"Wow. You sure are cranky-pants, huh?"

"Sorry, it's just that a butterfly never perched itself on my knee and started speaking to me before. I'm a little confused at the moment." I shake my head.

"Ok, ok, I get it. It's just that my master, Wizard Arbit Maximus, asked me to come and get you and take you back to Raiven with me. But, it's urgent; you have to come now."

Oh no. Wizard? What the... I make stopping gestures with both of my hands. "Whoa, whoa, whoa. Who is Ar...bee...it...Max...imus whatever?" I say trying to remember the name.

Sebastian lights up with the thought. "Wizard Arbit Maximus is the ruler of our world, Raiven—our world inside a rainbow. It's like a bridge between heaven and earth. It exists, and it is beautiful. It's a world with fairies, unicorns, mermaids, and even some evil creatures as well." He squints with fear. "Like trolls and very powerful, wicked witches. Well, one in particular." He pauses. "Um, your family won't even know you're gone—time does not exist there like it does here."

I narrow my eyes at him.

He flutters his wings again. "It's all true, I promise. And these creatures are as real as you and even me." Sebastian chuckles, and because he's so small, his whole body quivers. "Some people on Earth have claimed to see these creatures, because on occasion, they cross over from our dimension to yours...on missions. And many of our fairies and elves watch over and protect all of Earth's nature. Even though they are supposed to remain unseen, humans sometimes still can catch a glimpse."

"Go on."

He continues. "See, it's really in your world, but more like somewhat parallel to it, just in a different dimension. So, we can come in and out of it whenever we choose. It just vibrates at a higher frequency level. That's why you can't see us, and that's why time does not exist."

I tilt my head to one side. It amazes me that this world seems so much like the one I was talking about that day with Josie Lee on the patio swing. *I wonder if somehow the universe did hear our wish.* I pinch myself. Yet, nothing, other than some throbbing pain.

"It's kind of like a humming bird's wings—they flap so fast, the human eye can't see them, but you know they're there." Sebastian mimics this action then perches himself on my knee again. He looks directly into my eyes with a gentle smile upon his tiny face. "But, sometimes, if your heart is open, your guard is down, and you're in the moment, you just may see one of us, peeking at you from behind a tree or flower."

All of a sudden, I get flashbacks of that shadowy figure that kept appearing to me.

"Why can't you just make yourselves known to us?" I ask, turning my palms upwards. "I mean, really, what's the big deal?"

He lowers his tiny head. "Unfortunately, our kind feels that humans can be too self-destructive. We feel that if humans knew about our world or found a way to access it, they might find a way to destroy it forever. I mean, after all, they have found ways to destroy their own planet and even one another."

"But, why would we want to do that? Destroy your world, I mean?" I ask, kind of with hurt feelings. *I am one of those 'humans' afterall.*

"People do things out of fear—I guess the unknown is a scary thing to some."

My hands grab my hips. "Yeah, well, if we're so 'self-destructive', why would you need a *human's* help?"

He bats his feather-like, little eyelashes at me. "Because, you're *the one*."

"What do you mean, 'the one'? 'The one' for what?"

"The one who is supposed to save our world and change yours...*forever.*"

I flick Sebastian away from my leg and prop back up. "Wait a minute. Just hold on there. What do you mean, 'save your world or mine?' Me? Lil' ol' me?" The psychic's words bounce back in my head. *Something really significant is going to happen that is going to help you both 'save the world.'* I pace.

The rain stops, but it doesn't stop dripping from tree leaf to tree leaf. The birds come out from hiding and begin their chirping chorus. A small glistening of sunlight peers through two oak trees to the floor of the forest right next to us.

"Do you remember when you and your best friend wished upon a shooting star together? And what that wish was?" Sebastian asks.

Just hearing those words gives me a twinge in my belly. "Yes, of course, I do. But nothing ever came from it. It wasn't real, I guess." I reply.

Sebastian clears his throat. "Ah-hum. Not true. That's why I'm here to get you, because it did come true. You see, our world has been waiting for someone like you and your friend to make that wish for a very long time. It's destiny."

I look at Sebastian and lower my head with a frown. "And Josie Lee? What about her?"

"I'm sorry about your friend, Seraphina, and that she's not here with you any longer—in the physical sense that is. But, her death—there's a bigger reason for it, and soon you will see what that reason is. She will be with you, just in a different way—in a much more powerful way—in spirit." The beautiful butterfly dashes around my head as his wings make a marvelous trail of swirling colors.

A sort of calm washes over me, because I've never thought about it that way before.

"I know not everything makes complete sense to you now.

But, I promise if you come with me, it will in time. But, we need to go. There's no more time to spare." He's still fluttering close around my face with all his amazing colors. I'm almost cross-eyed trying to observe them all.

I stand still, placing my hand over my mouth. All the nature around me seems peaceful. I'm jealous of it for a minute. "I don't know, Sebastian, if I can go. I mean what about my family or school? I don't think..."

He interrupts. "I told you already. Time does not exist there like here. So, they won't even know the difference." He pauses, his wings slowing down a bit. "You *will* get to see her again."

I freeze. "Who?"

"Josie Lee," he whispers.

"What? But, how?"

"I told you. She's with you in spirit. And we have the means for you two to communicate with each other. Our world is that middle-ground between heaven and earth. And we've got the magic. She'll be guiding you, along with some others." Sebastian forms a thin line, which resembles a grin on his miniature face.

I cry as I fall to the floor. When I saw her in the hospital room, it was real—that beautiful girl in the hospital room dressed in a white, long, sparkling glitter-gown. "Really? You wouldn't lie to me?"

Sebastian flits around my body. "I would never lie to you. Really. She's waiting on you. She wants you to say you'll do it. Now, please, please, get up and stop crying. I hate crying."

I get up off the floor and wipe my tears, looking at him straight in the face. "Ok, I'll do it."

The sunshine beams out from behind the clouds.

IN FRONT OF MY EYES, is the most brilliant, massive

rainbow I have ever seen in my life. I gasp. It's magnificent with the most vibrant, rainbow colors. It shines so bright, it almost blinds me—I can't even look at it directly.

Flying over to it and getting in front of me, Sebastian swiftly turns his tiny frame around. "Stand back a minute."

A leprechaun guards the entrance along with his huge pot of gold. It glows a bright shimmery gold. It's so alluring it makes you almost want to swim in it. He has a long, red beard and pale skin. His top hat is green, which matches his velvet green jacket. His shoes are black, patent-leather and pointy. He takes a step back and puts out his arm to guard it. "Ah, what can I have ya' for today?" he asks with a strong accent. "What be ya' business heyr'? Ya' all stay away from me gold na',ya' heyr?"

Sebastian flutters his wings with rapid movement, moving up and down in the air. "No, no, we don't have any business with your gold, Sir Leprechaun. We just want to enter the rainbow to Raiven. I live here, and I'm bringing in with me a special guest."

The leprechaun looks at Sebastian, scratching his reddish beard. "Ooh, ok then. I heyr ya', me lad. What be the magic ward then to enta'?"

Sebastian clears his throat, then bellows out one with four syllables. "Far-vet-nug-in."

From there, the leprechaun stands to the side, and a magical, wooden door appears before us, which has to be about twelve feet tall; it has a huge, shiny, gold knocker.

Sebastian whistles three, high-pitched notes and then orders the knocker to knock three times. *Knock, knock, knock*—the loud sounds pulsate throughout the atmosphere. The door glides and creaks open.

Standing on the other side of it is a small, three-foot, fairy boy. His hair is platinum blonde and short, and his eyes are a sparkling emerald green. He has no shirt on, but is covered below with some sort of hand-woven cloth. His ears are pointy, and he's also barefoot. A bow and arrow hang around his shoulder, and his wings are clear and iridescent. His peach-colored skin glitters and glistens in the sunlight. *Breathtaking!*

A chill runs through my whole body. I quiver, feeling all warm and tingly inside. My nose is held high in the air from the strong aroma of gardenias. *There it is, again.* "It's you. From the hospital."

He nods, grinning.

"Why do I feel like that? And what's that amazing smell?"

Sebastian giggles.

Looking at Sebastian, "What? What's so funny?"

"It's just a joy to watch a human's response to Noah. The chills are from his strong magical presence, and he always smells like gardenias." Sebastian says examining my facial expression. "It's his trademark. Every fairy has their own. It's quite lovely, isn't it?"

I'm still staring at Noah; I can't take my eyes off of him. "It's always been you, hasn't it?"

He nods at me again. Then he smiles toward Sebastian. "Well, it's about time, my little friend. Where have you been? We've been waiting on you two." He speaks with a light, airy voice. It's not a boy voice or a girl voice; rather it's just neutral in tone.

Sebastian flaps around Noah's face. "Let's just say it took much convincing." He sneers and then flies toward me. "Seraphina, I'm happy to introduce you to your guide and warrior fairy, Noah. He has been with you your whole life, watching over. Not just you, but Josie Lee too. As a matter of fact, he's been with both of you in many past lifetimes as well."

"Wow." There's not much else to say, or I can't even put it into words.

"He will lead the way, all the way, and protect you." Sebastian says.

I look at Noah and reach out my hand to shake two of his fingers. "Nice to meet you, Noah."

Noah takes a step back and then bows. "The pleasure is all mine, my dear lady. Even though I know you already. You just don't remember. But I always do." His smile now reaches from one ear to the other.

I can't help but laugh. "A talking butterfly and a warrior-fairy." I plant my hand to my mouth and try and cover-up the snickering. "Toto, I have a feeling we're not in Kansas anymore."

They both look at me confused, not getting the joke. I stand up straight, more lady-like. "Never mind. Sorry. It's just a line from one of my favorite movies."

Noah extends his arm, gesturing for me to enter first. "After you, my dear lady."

I enter. Behind my head flies Sebastian. Noah follows behind us as well. The huge, wooden door closes with a loud *bang*. Inside the rainbow to Raiven we go. The minute I step through, I become dry. *Whoa! My eyes can't believe what I'm seeing. For crying out loud...*

CHAPTER EIGHT

Fairyland

MY EYES SCAN some of the most vibrant, green grass, which covers the hills and valleys like sheets of paper. A small fairy *swooshes* by my ear, and I peer up to take notice, not just of one, but many of them, flying around everywhere—swarms of them, all different colors and sizes. Some of them have blonde hair, some brown, some long, some short—male and female. My eyes don't know whether to stay focused on the fairies or to be careful not to step all over the array of flowers, enveloping the grass like a blanket; from lilies and gardenias, to sunflowers and roses. Many of the flowers are even multi-colored like crystals. I have never seen anything like it before.

It seems the male fairies wear just bottoms, made out of some cloth-like material, ranging in colors, and the females wear short, silky dresses. One sleeve seems to be missing on most of the dresses, covering just one shoulder. The dresses are multi-colored, flowing and shimmering, and all of the fairies' bodies glitter and sparkle. *It's just spectacular!*

One lands on my shoulder—a cute little female with short, chocolate brown hair and violet eyes. She whispers something in my ear. I can't make it out; it sounds like gibberish. *Goodness Gracious! Her smell is delicious.* It's a cross between baked oatmeal-raisin cookies and, like, jasmine and lavender with a hint of vanilla. There are so many wonderful blends of smells in this place that I can't even make them all out. Kind of reminds me of that little nurse in the hospital room that day. Now I know; really just a messenger sent from here.

The valleys seem to go on for miles. So, when I stare out to the horizon with my hand, blocking the sun because it's so bright in my eyes, I observe tiny cottages that seem to line up and stack along the way. My guess is that they're probably homes to many of these fairies, and in the very far distance to the horizon, sits a blue and white castle. I barely make out the sight, but I can still get a glimpse of the massive amounts of ivy that have attached themselves to it.

Pointing in that direction, I ask Noah. "What is that?"

Noah looks in the distance at the structure. "That, my dear lady, is the castle where Queen Ivy resides—she rules over all of fairy land here, has the most magical powers over all the fairies, and all order here must pass through her first."

I swallow hard, "Sounds pretty powerful."

He chuckles. "Oh, my dear lady, you have no idea just how powerful she can be."

I look down at Noah and smile. "Please, Noah, call me Seraphina."

"Oh. Ok. Sorry, my dear...I mean, Seraphina. Surely." Noah nods his head. "That's actually where we are headed. I will try and explain some things to you. I'm sure you must have many questions and thoughts flooding your mind. Yes?" His mouth forms a crooked smile.

"Uh-huh. I guess you could say that." I reply.

"Ok, well, just follow me, Seraphina, I will lead the way." He pauses for a second. "What would you like to know about first?" His walk is effortless, more like a glide.

"May I suggest you take your shoes off here?" He gestures at his bare ones." The grass is simply marvelous on your feet." His toes wiggle and sink more and more into the green bliss.

I take off my shoes, following Noah through fields of grass and flowers. My feet dig into the silkiness of the rich green, which seeps in between my toes too. "Wow, it is quite wonderful, I have to admit." I frolic through it.

"So?" He presses me.

Prancing through the hills as I follow Noah, he keeps reaching out his small hand to help me through the declines and valleys. "So, tell me more about Queen Ivy. Cause I feel like I've heard of her from somewhere before."

"Oh? And where might that have been?" he asks.

"Not sure. But, I feel like I'm having déjà vu. Call me crazy."

"Hmm. I would never call you 'crazy.'" His mouth forms a straight line. "But, maybe our worlds have crossed paths before. And your brain is having some sort of recollection."

"I didn't really mean that you would call me 'crazy.'" I shake my head. I look at Noah who seems confused. "Never mind."

It's in this moment that I realize this communication thing may be much harder than it seems. We are from different worlds and from different kinds, after all.

We continue walking toward the blue and white stone castle. Sebastian is quiet, following behind with flickering, colorful wings, allowing Noah to do all the talking.

Walking through the green grass along the beautiful valleys, we're getting closer and closer to the queen's castle. All the fairies are swarming around us as we walk. One even comes close to me, stops in mid-air, flapping her light pink wings, and plants a small kiss on my cheek. It catches me off-guard, and I almost trip in my tracks.

Noah chuckles again. "See, they are all grateful to you for coming. They realize the significance of you being here."

We walk down into a valley, past a creek with water running through it. Big, black stones scatter everywhere throughout its long distance. It must run miles and miles. I can't help but dip my feet into it.

"Why do they all seem to be in such a hurry?" I ask, referring to the fairies, scurrying and flying around everywhere.

"Well, they all have work to do for the queen—each equally vital. Fairies here don't see themselves as more important than the other. It's not like humans. They all feel and know their purpose and are happy to fulfill it. They take their jobs very seriously. Plus, fairies just move swiftly." He giggles with his arms folded behind his back. He's so confident when he speaks.

"Wow," I respond, becoming more and more mesmerized by the flowing water as we stroll. "That's awesome. I wish it were like that where I come from."

Noah jumps on a stone, clutching it like a pro. You can tell he is use to the feeling of nature on his bare feet.

Watching his playfulness, I'm somewhat envious that he can feel that way at a time like this. I wonder if he always has this all-is-well mind frame.

"Tell me more about the queen. Please."

"Well, what would you like to know about her exactly?" he asks as he focuses on his hopping game from stone to stone without getting wet.

"Is she nice?" I ask.

Noah giggles again. This seems to be his common response to me. It's beginning to make me feel like an idiot. Blood rushes to the surface of my face.

"Yes. Most fairies are. We have much respect for others. You have nothing to fear," he replies with a slight wave of his hand.

"If everyone is pretty much equal, why a queen?" I fold my arms. I feel that's a pretty smart question. *Ha. Now laugh.*

"Ah, good question," he remarks.

My arms unfold. Now, I'm interested.

He continues while springing like a little frog from stone to stone. "Well, to keep rule and order over our land. Otherwise, the fairies would be lost. We keep and value many, many years of tradition here, which must be maintained."

"Ok, that makes sense. So, what does she want from me?" I walk through the creek next to him, not being able to resist getting my feet wet in this awesome water flow.

He stops jumping and turns to look at me. "Well, to get back the rainbow crystal, of course." Then, he turns to face Sebastian at this point. "You didn't tell her?"

"Well...I...I didn't get a chance to," Sebastian stutters, sounding a bit panicky. "I had to get her to come. I don't know if she would have hearing that." He swooshes down by a stone near Noah's feet, peering up at him with pleading eyes. "Please don't be upset."

"Calm down, my little friend. It's ok." He bends down to pat Sebastian's wing, then stands back up and looks at me. "Sometimes our little friend here gets worked up."

Noah and I snicker at the same time. I'm finally on his page.

"So?" I ask.

"So..." he hesitates briefly. "So, it was stolen by the evil witch, Alyssa, and her trolls," he continues. "You see..." he rubs his small chin from side to side. "By Alyssa stealing the crystal, she will look and remain young forever."

"If she's a witch, can't she just cast a spell to make that happen, and then this whole thing is caput?" I wave my hand.

"Well, not exactly." His shoulders shrug, and his head tilts to one side.

"Why not? Do I even want to know what you're going to say next?" I flinch.

He takes a deep breath. "The crystal gives her the power to rule over all of Raiven. She will then turn this place into a blundering hellfire pit, which will basically be like her paradise. So, in order to save Raiven from complete and utter chaos and destruction, you must get the crystal back from Alyssa, and then return it to its owner—the great and powerful wizard, Arbit Maximus, to whom it belongs and where they stole it from. You're the only one who has the power now to do that. Phew." He lets out his breath.

Again, I'm starting to feel like I'm in the movie *The Wizard of Oz*. I gawk at Noah with my mouth hanging wide open. "Excuse me, what?"

"Didn't know that part either, I guess, huh?" Noah scratches the bottom of his chin.

He sounds like a teacher from one of my classrooms. That's how they would react if I didn't understand my work assignment.

Planting my hands on my hips, "Um, no. All I know is something about Wizard Arbit Maximus needed Sebastian to come get me. That it was urgent. I didn't realize what that urgency meant."

"Yes, my dear...I mean, Seraphina. He needs you alright. He needs you to save Raiven. And that's what Queen Ivy and I will assist with. The queen has the powers and the map of Raiven to help you do that. She has lived thousands of years, longer than anyone here, or any wizard. Nobody knows this place better."

I point to myself with a puzzled look. "But, why am *I* the only one with the power?"

"Because *you* made the wish, which opened the doorway

between ours and yours. It doesn't happen very often. It is a rarity." He pokes me in my chest. "You're our only hope."

Sebastian is flapping around our heads. "Please, Seraphina, please help us. You must."

This can't really be happening. I must be dreaming. I'm waiting to be pinched. Flustered from the inside out, I puff out a large, long breath. "Goodness Gracious." I mumble, clapping my hand over my mouth. "Yes, I guess I did, didn't I?" And for the first time, this all hits me like a ton of bricks. It's too much to take in. I fall to my knees, splashing the water. *This is really happening. I am the chosen one.*

WE ARRIVE at the ivy-covered castle, which is so much more magnificent up-close. The white stone sparkles in the light, glittering. There is a round pond in the front with lily pads and lotus flowers, and it's surrounded by an incredible garden of so many different white flowers, which I don't even know the names of. I raise my nose high in the air and inhale deeply. "Ooh."

Noah agrees. "I know; it's splendid. But, you actually get used to it after a while."

"Well, I could enjoy getting used to it then." My nose is still raised in the air.

A soft breeze blows a loose strand of hair into my face. There are not many trees around, but the flowers and hedges sway and rustle. The weather is in the low seventies (at least, that's what it feels like) —there's not a cloud in the sky. Seems pretty perfect to me. "Is it always like this outside here?"

"Most of the time," Noah gleams. He gestures toward the door of the castle. "Shall we?"

"Ahem, before you do..." Sebastian clears his throat. We

almost forgot about him, flapping his tiny wings around both of us. "Excuse me, I do not mean to interrupt, but this is where I leave you, Seraphina." He frowns. *It's so cute on him.*

I look directly into Sebastian's tiny eyes. My belly has a twinge in it, because I don't want him to leave. It's something about his presence that just makes me more comfortable—maybe it is because he was the one who convinced me to come here.

"Why? What do you mean?" I ask as my hand rests on my lower belly. My eyes begin to water.

"Oh, please don't look at me like that. You know how I hate it when people cry. It makes me really jittery." His flying is all over the place.

"I just don't understand why you have to go?" I pout.

"Because my work here is done, and you are in good hands with Noah." He shoots Noah a smirk. "Plus, Queen Ivy is very particular about whom she lets inside her castle. You must go speak with her in private—she's been waiting on your arrival."

"Me?" I point to myself. "How does she know?"

"Because, again, you're the one." He *puffs* some air out of his mouth and tries to roll whatever little eyeballs he has. "Now go." Planting a miniature kiss on my nose, he flies away.

He fades away into the blue sky, but just before he does, the wind carries with it his last words. "I believe in you."

My gaze drifts from the sky back to Noah, where he is staring at me, waiting for my attention. "Are you ready now?"

"Yes," I say. "I'm actually going to miss him." I lift my hand from my belly, inhale deeply, and walk on.

THE LARGE, wooden door in front of us resembles the one we entered to go inside of Raiven; it slides open.

When it opens completely, standing there is a beautiful, long, sandy-haired, female fairy with pale skin and hazel eyes. *Are fairies always standing at the other side of an opening door here? Golly!* She wears a heart-shaped neckline and light-blue, short dress. A pearl necklace lies on her chest and ivy is wrapped around portions of her wrists, forearms, ankles, and calves. Her wings are marvelous—light blue at the base and blend into white at the tips. Rainbow-colored sparkles cover them all over. One arm bends at the elbow as the other rests by her side, her fingers pointing ever-so-slightly. A beam of light radiates from her smiling face. She is bigger than Noah, maybe around five-foot-five, but also barefoot. I don't think that any fairies own a pair of shoes here in Fairyland.

"Hello. Welcome to my sanctuary." Her voice is sweet and smooth like vanilla ice cream. She opens up her arms wide to greet me.

Looking over at Noah, I'm seeking his approval to approach her. He nods. I walk over to Queen Ivy. She wraps her arms around me and squeezes me, giving me the warmest, tightest hug I think I've ever received. Goosebumps invade my entire body.

"I have been waiting on you," Queen Ivy whispers in my ear. "Emm."

Her scent is more like a strong, flowery perfume. She smells like what I think a queen would smell like, if that makes *any* sense. If powerful, yet sweet has a scent.

Noah walks away into another room—off to the side—closing the door behind him, giving us our privacy, I would assume.

We stay like that for a few more seconds when Queen Ivy lets me go and stares straight into my eyes. Her soft hands relax on my shoulders. "Have you been looking forward to coming?"

I'm at a loss for words. "Umm. I guess. Not really sure."

She turns around and sashays away to the other side of the room.

"But, happy to be here now." I blurt out, hoping I didn't offend the royal highness.

Queen Ivy moves on as if she didn't even hear the comment. She sits down on a large, dark, wooden chair with ivy wrapped all around it and crosses one leg over the other; she reclines against the back of her throne with every movement in complete perfection. Her long, wavy hair drapes around her shoulders, extending right below her boobs. "Your work to be done here in Raiven is of the utmost importance and is not going to be easy. However, all of my fairies and I couldn't be more grateful for you coming and agreeing to this. We need your help to save our precious world."

Is that what I did? Yikes. I feel flattered to be considered so important, yet I still don't understand how I can be 'the one'? The thought is too much for my mind. But, they all seem to think I fit the bill. So, I'm here, not going anywhere, and most importantly, I really want to see Josie Lee again. *But, what's all this about it's, 'not going to be easy'?* I swallow hard.

"I'm sure this all must be very overwhelming for you," the queen continues. "Did Noah fill you in with any questions you may have?" She takes a sip of some sort of fizzing, pink-like champagne next to her throne. It has pink flower petals in it. "Would you like a glass?" She holds it up in the air for me to view better. "Makes you strong and powerful." Queen Ivy takes another sip.

"Oh, no thank you, I think I'm a little young to be drinking." I wave my hands.

This statement amuses the Queen because she throws her head back with a loud laugh. "No, no, no. We fairies do not drink alcohol or take any controlled substances here in Fairyland. We find euphoria in all that's natural. This is a special potion called, Potiona a la Mode. It's made with the finest berries, vegetables, and fruits—rich with the best vitamins and minerals for your mind, body, and soul. The fizzle comes from my magic pixie dust, and the lotus petals cool the body and enhance good health."

She takes out a small, blue-velvet pouch and removes a pinch of pixie dust, flicking more into the flute. The pink liquid simmers, bubbles, and fizzles some more. Her lips gently touch the top of the glass, taking another small sip. "Mmmm. The dust helps me keep up my magical powers; otherwise, I can become very drained of energy and fatigued. Then, I'm no good to any of my fairies around here. Plus, I am very old." She smacks her lips together.

Old? Hmm. You sure can't tell by the looks of her. She looks like about eighteen or something around that age. "Well, it looks tasty," I respond not knowing what else to say about a magic potion called, Potiona a la Whatever. *Can we get on with this already? For Pete's Sake.*

"It's ok, because I will be giving some of my magical pixie dust for you to take on your quest. It will stay and remain in the hands of Noah, so he can control the amount you will consume. It has many purposes and can be extremely powerful. A human cannot fully understand its benefits, and it can be dangerous to you if not used properly. But, it will help you in many different ways along your journey, including helping you communicate with your loved one who's passed...Josie Lee."

That's it...that's all I need to hear...those words...that name...*Josie Lee.* It echoes in my mind over and over. *Josie Lee...Josie Lee.*

"I am very sorry for your loss, by the way." Yet, here in our world the spirit is as real, alive, and nearer than you think. Humans haven't wrapped their complex brains around this theory yet—some more evolved than others, I guess." She uncrosses her legs. It occurs to me that speaking of humans may make Queen Ivy a little uncomfortable. *Or maybe it's me?* It seems like I'm the human alien here in Fairyland. *Wait. I am.*

Not knowing what else to do at that moment, I do what always feels comfortable to me—pick at my cuticles. "Great." I bestow a partial smile and peer at Queen Ivy, looking mighty powerful on her throne. "I'm ready."

"Good." The queen notices my bad habit. "You shouldn't do that. Not very flattering on such a pretty, young lady."

"Huh." I snort. "Sounds like someone I know. Yes, you're right." And it occurs to me that my best friend's presence is already near-by.

CHAPTER NINE

The Map

QUEEN IVY ORDERS and waves her hand up in the air as any queen would do to call out her duties. At least, I would assume. "Leila...Faye..." she calls.

Two, tiny fairies—maybe the size of the queen's hand—flurry over to me immediately. Both have a bright, florescent, yellow-green, glowing light. One has short, black hair with pointy ears and a slender face, while the other has short, blonde hair with a rounder face. Leila and Faye both carry in their tiny hands some sort of a map, and drop it in Queen Ivy's lap. They turn to fly away, but before they get the chance to hurry out, the queen stops them in their tracks.

"Now, now, little ladies, be nice to our guest and greet her please." They both stop and turn to face me in mid-air.

"Don't mind them, Seraphina. These two can be in quite a hurry at times, being they're very busy little bees for their queen. Let me introduce you to my fair pair, Leila..." The curly blonde smiles and slightly waves as her tiny cheeks redden.

"And Faye..." The black-haired beauty takes a bow. I notice that Faye has the most unique violet, slanted eyes I have ever seen, and that Leila's are bright sky-blue. Both fairies are superb looking. Then they scatter away without a word. The queen is beaming from ear to ear with their quick entrance and exit, which leaves behind a scent of like cinnamon and cupcakes.

"Those two are my right and left arms. I could not get my work done without them. And don't let their little sizes fool you, because they are powerful beyond measure. None more powerful than their queen, though," she finishes saying with a smirk.

She glances down at the map and picks it up, unrolling it until it opens. "So, Seraphina, this is the map you will need to take with you. This will be your main source that will let you know where you're going throughout Raiven, how to get back the rainbow crystal to return to Arbit Maximus, and some of the important symbols, landmarks, and then obstacles you may encounter along the way."

'Obstacles'? Gulp.

She stands up and walks over to me, taking me by the arm. "Come with me here—let's view it together."

Queen Ivy leads me over to a long, wooden-oak dining table and lays the map down on it; she places two crystal paper weights on the end of each side. They're fairy statues..

Laid out in front of my face is a bright, colorful map of what looks like the world of Raiven. On the bottom of the map is the door, which I entered Raiven from. Behind the green valley is a faint in the background, which reads, Queen Ivy's Castle in black, calligraphy-like ink. Throughout the valleys, the word *Fairyland* is written on the map. On top of the castle is what looks like some sort of a rainbow-colored vortex that swirls around, reaching all the way to the top of the map, connecting to another castle. It reads, Wizard Arbit Maximus's Castle & Rainbow Crystal.

The vortex starts with the red realm (evil realm), and then it goes up from there— orange realm (land of gigantic honey bees); yellow realm (land of sunshine and sunflowers); green realm (crystal forest of the elves); blue (water realm); violet (spiritual realm). Then, there's a big circle starting from the bottom of the queen's castle, which goes around and up the vortex, all the way back around to the other side of the map and back around to the castle. Following the circle, beginning to the left, which is the west (according to the map); there is an arrow, which goes through each realm – starting with the red up to the violet. The arrow, which looks like some sort of trail, crisscrosses through each realm—going west to east, east to west, until it reaches the highest realm of violet, stopping at Wizard Arbit Maximus's castle. However, at every border of every realm, there's a box drawn with the letter *D*.

Queen Ivy places her delicate finger on the picture of her castle. "We are here now in my castle. When you leave, you will go west, following this trail." She traces her finger along the black arrow, following a path on the map. "You will begin in the red realm—the evil realm—where Witch Alyssa lives and where you'll have to seize back the rainbow crystal from her and her evil trolls."

My mouth hangs open in disbelief. "But how?"

She notices the horror on my face. "Don't worry. I will explain to you how, but when the time is right. I want to get through your path first. You will have a powerful, warrior fairy with you and unicorn, whom you haven't met yet. They both will be protecting you."

I just nod my head. "Unicorn, really?" *What?* I'm trying to remain calm, yet my insides are running the Boston marathon.

"Yes, Seraphina, a unicorn...that you helped birth," responds the queen.

"Ahem," I clear my throat. "Excuse me, what?"

"When you and your friend, Josie Lee, made that wish together that starry night, you birthed a unicorn. You see, every time a human makes a wish to enter our world, a unicorn is born." The queen explains.

"Oh, does that happen often?" I laugh and throw my head back.

"No. It doesn't. Hasn't happened in over two hundred years. And because you made that wish, and birthed your unicorn, you gave yourself the power you needed to arrive here. Unfortunately, it's not under the most pleasant circumstances. But, thank goodness you did, because you were meant to come—it's your destiny."

"Why do I feel like I've heard this somewhere before?" I tilt my head to the side. "Maybe this time, I'll believe it." I crack a smile just trying to find a little humor in this crazy situation.

"Ok, so to finish," the queen continues, "after you get the crystal, you will head to this entryway to the orange realm (land of gigantic honey bees). This here is an invisible door to enter to the next upper realm. They all are invisible." That's when her sparkly fingernail points to the box with the letter *D* written in it. "However, your job is to find the door. And you will do that with the help of the pixie dust. When sprinkled on the door, it appears."

"Oooh-k. But how do I know how to find where the doors are?"

"That's the challenge. There are two, invisible doors in every realm—in the west and east sides." Queen Ivy is somewhat slouched with the map underneath her hands, looking at me. "And behind every one of these doors is a waterfall with a reflection of a rainbow." She now stands up straight and serious.

"Once you find the waterfall, you will find a door. You will throw a handful of the pixie dust at it in mid-air, and the door will appear." This action is mimicked with her hand. "Then, you will continue through each realm until you reach the violet realm—home of Wizard Arbit Maximus and his castle—to return the rainbow crystal back where it belongs.

"But, in order to enter through these doors, you must either have the magical powers of Raiven, which you don't, or have the rainbow crystal." She pauses staring at me for a moment and then grabs me by the shoulders. "You'll have the crystal...*hope-fully*." Queen Ivy smiles.

Here it is again. Like I'm in some sort of trippy dream. But, the only words that spill out from my mouth are, "Yeah, '*hopefully*.'"

"Are you ok, Seraphina?" She shakes me a little.

"This is just a lot to take in. It's all a bit, well, overwhelming, to say the least." I look down to the floor, feeling intimidated. "I'm just not sure I can do this."

The queen looks into my eyes. "You can and you will. And I'm going to tell you why you can...because, you are the chosen one."

I shrug my shoulders. "Ok," I say. "Yeah. Apparently. I keep hearing that. I wish I could reach for some sort of an exit door to run in the other direction and never look back. That's how I really feel – scared out of my mind. There's that rapid thumper heart-beat feeling again. I gnaw on my cuticle.

"Sorry to rush you through this, Seraphina, but we don't have much time. And I seem to have forgotten that I'm telling this to a ten-year-old human. It's not like I deal with humans on a regular basis, so please forgive my nature."

She embraces me with a warm hug.

I release a couple held-back tears down my cheeks.

"Do not be afraid, Seraphina. You must trust me."

Sure. Easy for her to say.

WHEN WE WALK outside the queen's glittering castle, we're greeted by hundreds of fairies gathered around. The sun is setting beautiful yellow, orange, purplish colors along the horizon. Some fairies are dancing around a medium-sized fire-pit, while others are holding hands and twirling around in the air as if celebrating something. A blonde, curly-haired, angelic-looking fairy wearing a long, flowing, pink dress plays the harp. A much smaller fairy boy flying in the air above my head is playing a flute. The combination is completely in synch and heavenly—if heaven has a song.

"Wow," I say.

"It's getting dark. Now is a time for celebration and then rest before your great quest tomorrow." Queen Ivy caresses my hands with hers. "Here in Fairyland everything is to be celebrated, because life is a gift. So, when one ventures out on an important task, we celebrate. When one is born, we celebrate, and when one passes on, we celebrate. We say, 'pass on' because there is no such thing as death." Now, she somewhat squeezes my hands. "It's just transcendence into a higher dimension—the highest one there is—our home with God." Releasing my hands, she lifts hers up as if pointing to the heavens. She looks up, closes her eyes, and inhales deeply with a calm grin.

Noah looks at his queen and beams.

I focus in on Queen Ivy soaking in her words and gestures, and then watch all the lovely fairies, embracing and enjoying the moment—enjoying their precious 'gift of life' as the queen said.

Queen Ivy looks at her fairies in Fairyland, and then back at me, walking away. "Go, enjoy yourself."

Noah plants a gentle hand on my arm as we walk together toward the celebration taking place.

"Seraphina?" Queen Ivy calls me from behind. "One last thing before I send you off tomorrow."

I turn around. "What's that?"

"Remember. You're in a higher frequency here, so don't be surprised if your dreams are vivid. Sometimes we leave our bodies while we sleep or astral travel, and we can even receive messages from spirit or higher powers." She waves like a delicate beauty pageant winner, turns around, and walks back inside to her castle—one leg graciously flowing in front of the next like she is floating on a cloud.

"Umm, ok, anything else?" I mumble aloud, not really seeking an answer, just trying to make sense of it all. "I mean, could this place be any more bizarre? Talking butterflies, invisible doors, unicorns, powerful witches and wizards. It's as if I'm in some sort of epic fantasy movie or something." I shake off a chill.

"I am here by your side, Seraphina, to help you through this," Noah's hand pats my arm. It feels warm and homey like melted butter on my English muffin. "I will not leave you. I have sworn to my queen to take care of you til' the end, and I will do my very best to hold up my end of the deal."

I look over at Noah with a grateful smile; I believe him. "Thank you."

CHAPTER TEN

An Amazing Dream

NOAH, two other fairies, and I sit around a burning fire pit, taking turns sipping fresh spring water out of little, leaf-like tea cups. The fairy boy with dark purple hair and Noah are even drinking that potion stuff in champagne flutes like their queen. They pass around a plate of berries, nuts, and small, warm cinnamon buns that have been roasting by the fire pit. I bite into one, and it's so warm and moist. A drip of tasty syrup runs down the side of my mouth, and I lick it off with one swipe of my tongue. "Mmm."

The musical instruments of the fairies passing by continue to play as the air carries its tunes. It sounds like some sort of a Renaissance festival—being I've been before in the past with Josie Lee. She loved going, getting all into it.

There are different sounds, like the harp, flute, violin, cello, and instruments I've never quite heard before; one even looks like a miniature harp—*so cute*.

There are a few fairies telling old stories and folklore

about their people and their world of Raiven. Some are so great and wondrous, I can't help but snicker. The fairy boy with short, dark, purple hair and a long, bony nose tells a tale of his baby sister fairy who was birthed out of a white rose bud.

I look at Noah in disbelief; he chuckles at me. "Anything in Raiven is possible. It's magic."

"Yeah. I'm starting to see that," I respond.

Then another girl fairywith long, red curly hair tells of her one true-love-fairy, Ariston, who fought in a battle with one of the witch's trolls, and was shot and killed with his poisonous arrows. Small tear drops roll down her cheeks as she speaks of him.

But the mood changes again with a funny story of another fairy boy who was chased down by a deer in attempt to kill it for its meat. Apparently, the fairy boy ran for the hills. Everyone around the fire pit laughs. He explains to me that his is an uncommon occurrence in Fairyland because most of them are vegans; they don't believe in the murdering or eating of any animal or its parts. Yet, there are a few exceptions of fairies who still do, usually the ones who harvest their grounds and gardens, believing that the meat makes them bigger, leaner, and stronger for the job at hand.

It is now completely dark outside. I can't tell what time it is. Maybe nine or ten o'clock? But still not sure. It doesn't seem like anyone around here tells time or is even interested. It's not like I've seen a clock, or any of the fairies wear watches. They just are all constantly in the moment—it's quite an unbelievable thing that they can do that. Actually, it's so cool that I don't have to worry about being in bed at a certain time for once. Just as that thought enters my mind, I think about the challenges I will be facing as soon as tomorrow. Those annoying chills run up and down my spine. I can't bear to think about it. I just want to be like my fairy friends around the fire pit and enjoy the moment for what it is.

"So, what's the deal with this witch lady, Alyssa, anyway?" I interrupt the conversation with my question—almost immediately regret asking it when I see the look of puzzlement on their faces, but it's like I couldn't help myself; it just spilled out.

The dark, purpled-hair fairy looks at Noah. "You didn't tell her?"

Noah responds, "I did. Well, maybe just filled her in a bit." He picks some grass next to his feet. "I didn't want to overwhelm her all at once."

The other two fairies gasp for air. They're talking about me for a minute like I'm not even here.

For Pete's sake...why doesn't anyone around here ever give me the whole story?

Then, they look at Noah and both say in complete harmony, "Well, now's your chance."

"Ok. It's complicated, Seraphina." He turns to me; we're both sitting with our legs crossed. I can see the reflection of the fire pit's flames in Noah's pupils as he speaks. "There is good and evil in this world, and the two are always battling each other."

Again, another déjà vu echoes in my mind.

"Alyssa is part of that evil," he goes on to explain.

"And don't forget those terrifying, ugly creatures that associate themselves with her—those treacherous trolls," the red-haired fairy adds, "those things are pure evil."

Not acknowledging her comments, Noah continues to explain to me. "It can't be explained why some choose this path, but maybe the purpose of free will is so one can choose. One cannot know good without bad."

I glug down some spring water out of my tea cup. "Yeah, but, why steal the crystal? I mean, can't she just be evil from her realm and mind her own business, living happily ever after with those troll thinga-ma-jingas?"

"Ahhh," the black-haired fairy raises his pointer finger in the air, "but what would be the fun in that? Too boring for her."

"I thought I explained it to you. So, she can stay and look young forever. She's obsessed with her own outer beauty. Ego and external power can ruin anyone, Seraphina. It becomes its own life force and can take over."

"Too bad she's not concerned about the inner part," the red-haired fairy spits out.

Noah nods in agreement. "But mainly, to rule over all of Raiven. And not just Raiven, but your world too. Eventually, she will take over Raiven, and then planet Earth is second in line. Our two worlds are one-in-the-same. We're all connected."

"But how? Why?" I cringe.

She wants it all. All the power, I guess. And we can't let her win," the red-haired fairy says. "We have to stop her."

"Once Alyssa gets her full power restored from the crystal and some other things," he gulps, "then she'll be able to control Raiven. After Raiven is under her power, she will be able to enter in and out of Raiven and Earth anytime with no boundaries."

At this point, my knees are up to my ears. I wrap my arms tight, squeezing in my legs close to my chest, and I rest one side of my head on one of them, listening. "But, can't Wizard Arbit Maximus just stop her?"

"No. He loses a lot of his powers without the crystal. See, it restores and empowers those who have it in their possession." Noah adds.

I jitter and sit up and can't help but bite my thumb cuticle. "When you said, 'and some other things'...what did you mean exactly?"

Again, Noah *gulps*, but this time it's so loud, they all hear it.

"Yeah, I was afraid you'd ask that." He glances down at the ground, picks up some of the potion, and takes a big sip. "Ok. Here it goes."

"What? Tell me." I say, now chomping on my cuticles.

"In order for her to take complete control..." he pauses for a long silence.

"Yeah?" I prod him.

"She must sacrifice the unicorn—presenting him with its magical horn—and kill 'the chosen one' to appease her evil god."

"What? 'The chosen one'?" Pointing to my chest, "Aren't I the 'chosen one'?" This time it's my hard *gulp* that everyone hears, and I can feel my eyeballs grow to the size of saucers. My feet go numb. They must've fallen asleep under my knees. At this point, it feels like thousands of tiny spiders are scurrying around everywhere inside of them, pinching me.

Noah and I are now staring into each other's eyes. The burning flame reflection still blazing in them. "Yes, my dear, you are," he says. "And only the chosen one has the power to get the crystal back. Our fate and yours, and the fate of your people, all depend on you."

"Oh. No pressure or anything." I bite the loose piece of cuticle, hanging from my thumb again. Every hair on my body is now standing up straight and tall like little soldiers in an army.

How do I live up to that?

THAT SAME NIGHT, after all the exhausting conversation around the fire pit, I perch myself under a large willow tree to take in everything from that day.

From a short distance away, Noah is still making small-talk with some of the fairies around the fire. He glances at me to make sure I'm ok. Taking notice of him, I just give him a slight wave so he knows I could use a moment to myself. He turns back around to engage in continuous conversation.

The moon is so gigantic it lights up the whole sky. It sits right on the line of the horizon as if it were painted there by someone. The stars are also magnificent; like huge twinkling, sparkling diamonds in the sky. The black sky is so clear—no clouds, no Milky Way; just pure, black perfection around them. The stars even seem closer.

Everything here in Raiven seems that much more beautiful than on Earth itself, although Raiven is still somewhat on planet Earth—I can't really wrap my head around how that works yet. *Like, where does this place actually exist?*

My mind drifts, staring at this remarkable view with the sound of crickets chirping in the night-air. My eyes become heavy; I can't keep them open any longer. I wonder how this is all possible. *How am I going to save Raiven, get the crystal back, and then save my own planet?* But the thought is just too overpowering. It seems like an impossible journey. I will just have to tell the queen and Noah in the morning that I can't do it. Plus, I want to go home—I'm starting to miss my family, and I haven't even seen Josie Lee. The thought is too unbearable anymore; I fall into a deep sleep.

FLOATING ABOVE MY BODY, I look down at myself, sleeping under the willow tree. Noah lies next to me, sleeping as well. He must have laid a knitted blanket over me because one now covers me. I'm on my side with my head perched under my hands as if to make a pillow. Stuffed leaves gather under Noah's head. Both of us look very peaceful. A jolting feeling shoots through my body. It occurs to me that I'm having an out-of-body experience, and I'm feeling extremely weightless and free. *Am I*

dead? No, I must be dreaming. Well, if this is a dream, then I can do anything I want. The thought passes through my mind. *Yes, I can. So, I will fly— fly to the beautiful moon and diamonds in the sky. Whoosh!* I take off, soaring through the black night.

My eyes are closed, feeling and hearing the cool breeze, *swooshing* through my hair and chilling my cheeks. I'm not afraid of where I'm going. It doesn't matter; nothing bad can happen to me. Plus, it's my dream—I can do whatever I want with it. Nothing can or will harm me; I'm in total control. My arms are out like an airplane, and I suddenly open my eyes to find myself perched and stopped directly in front of that massive moon; grayish silver with craters the size of football fields. I can reach out my hand and touch it, but don't want to for some reason. It's too vulnerable for me, like I would be invading its space somehow. It dawns on me that the moon may be allowing me to look at it, with its amazing grace, and I'm not to disrespect its immaculate presence; I'm grateful for it.

The light of its illumination is so powerful, yet it doesn't blind me. *Is it a God of some sort? Is God trying to tell me something?* It feels like it on some level. The only thought that bounces into my mind right when I ask myself those two very questions is *go play amongst the stars, and do with them whatever you like. Awesome!*

I soar straight up high above to the stars. Even though I'm in space, I can still see below me—Noah sleeping under the willow tree. It's as if I've left the atmosphere, but I really haven't; somehow, I'm still here.

Stopping in mid-air, I view the sparkling diamonds in the sky. I take one and place it where I want. Then, I take another, putting it next to the first, then another next to another, until I form my own pictures— my very own constellations. I make shapes like hearts, half-moons, and butterflies. *This is so cool!*

After tiring of this game for a while, I decide it's time to go back to my body. I land down next to myself, and observe the peacefulness on my face one last time. Questioning going back inside my body—to a place of boundaries and gravity—I hesitate for a moment. Then, something incredible happens.

An apparition forms a huge figure of some sort. I can't make out who or what, but then it starts to take on its shape: a long, white-bearded, old, dark-brown, colored man with a large, wooden stick, which must be the size of his own ten-foot body. He has one blue eye and one green one, with hundreds of wrinkles upon his wise, old face. Smiling at me, he wears a velvet, dark-blue, pointed hat and matching cloak. I don't feel fear at all. If anything, I feel a warm, loving feeling; I even get goose bumps. *That's happening to me a lot lately.*

"Don't hesitate. You must go back to yourself." He points his stick toward my sleeping body on the ground and then glowers at me. "Never fear, I am always near-by, sweet child. Just remember yourself always like in this dream, and there will be nothing you can't achieve. You will be alright."

As fast as the large, old man appears, is as fast as he disappears.

"Wait," I call out to him. "Who...are...you?"

But it is too late. He is already gone.

Glancing back at my sleeping body, I feel differently this time. Yes, he's right. I must go back.

CHAPTER ELEVEN

Pixie Dust, Tea, and the First Glimpse of a Ghost

I WAKE under the willow tree to sunshine, peering through its openings, and a light, crisp breeze on my face. I sit up, yawn, and stretch my arms high in the air. "Ahh. I was so tired last night. I must have just passed out. I slept like a baby."

"I didn't want to move you into the castle and wake you. You looked so peaceful." Noah says, sitting next to me as if he was just waiting for me to rise.

I yawn again with my hand over my mouth, mumbling, "Didn't you sleep?"

"I did, a bit," he responds. "But, we fairies don't need as much sleep as humans. Our energy is not as drained as yours. Human energy consists of a lot. You take more from one another. It's not like that here for us. We just average about three to four hours of sleep a night, and that's it. I've been up for a while, waiting on you."

"Oh, I'm sorry. I didn't—"

"Please," he interrupts. "Don't be sorry, my dear. One thing

I do have is patience. I could sit here all day with no worries or nowhere to go." He grins with content.

"Really?" I question. "Well, that's def a talent in my book." I bite a cuticle on my index finger—something about his perfectionism and all these fairies here in Fairyland kind of drives me nuts sometimes. I feel insecure, like humans are some sort of a lesser race. *Who knows, maybe we are?* Sometimes it does feel like I roam the planet with a bunch of whackos anyway. My face scrunches up with the thought.

"You ok?" Noah asks.

"Oh, yeah." I nod and shrug. I don't want to let him on, knowing that this could be true. Better to keep it a secret. I've got to somehow get this into my thick skull that I can do this, and this is no time for any signs of doubting myself. Maybe it's better to prove him wrong; maybe humans aren't getting enough of the credit they deserve. Yeah, maybe not. *Who's to say that one ten-year-old human girl couldn't save the planet from complete destruction?*

"What do you say we head back to Queen Ivy's castle? Have some morning tea and breakfast to get us started on our way?" Noah asks.

"Um, sure. I guess. Sounds good." I am hungry.

We both get up from the rich, green grass and cross the path that leads back to the queen's castle.

I feel the warmth of the sun's rays as I glance up at the sky and notice that it's as clear as it was the day I arrived: cool and crisp as ever. The weather conditions seem like complete perfection to go along with the smells here. It constantly smells like a combination of oatmeal cookies baking in the oven, yet there's a hint of perfume scents to go along with it. It's like I get a free pass to Disney World without the crowds and long lines. *Hallelujah!*

The second that we arrive at the queen's door, it opens and

she's standing there with her dazzling presence to go along with it. Her arms are out ready to embrace me again for the second time, squeezing me in a hug. "There you are. I wanted to let you get your beauty rest, for today begins a new journey, so I knew you would need it. How did you sleep?"

I can't understand how she asks me this so nonchalantly as if it were my wedding day or something.

I rub my eyes, still somewhat waking up. "I actually slept better than I can ever remember. I had a really amazing dream." The memory of it makes me beam with delight.

"I told you. Here they are extraordinary and meaningful. Expect to receive messages only you can understand." She waves down Leila and Faye. "Ladies, fetch us some tea and warm croissants please." Although it's a command, it's not really demanded. It's accepted when it's the queen, yet she still requests it in a respectable manner.

Queen Ivy puts her arm around me. "Come, let's take a walk. We'll have tea and breakfast in my garden today," she says grinning from ear to ear.

The three of us stroll together through the queen's stone walls of the castle. They sparkle as we pass them by. We reach French double doors with white borders. She presses down on the handles, and both doors swing open. What lies in front of us is something quite eye-catching; a sight that makes me gasp.

The whole backyard is a large, open space with all the beautiful nature one could ever take in. We go sit on a circular, stone bench that matches the exterior of the castle. It glitters in the sunlight. Surrounding us on each side are two huge, oak trees. A refreshing breeze brushes my face and blows my hair a bit. I hold my face up to it and meet the perfect rays of sunlight.

There's a curvy, stone pathway that leads to the bench, and on each side of the path are butterfly gardens. Every type of butterfly surrounds us—from the Monarch butterfly to aqua blue and black and even bright, yellow ones. Some are even multi-colored like Sebastian.

Butterflies flutter in my belly thinking about Sebastian again, and what lies ahead. I miss Sebastian, wondering if I'll ever see the little, frantic fellow who introduced me to this complicated, yet wondrous place again.

There are also rose gardens—mainly white roses—but there are also pink and yellow ones as well. We sit at the bench, which is underneath a pergola. The pergola is stark white with ivy wrapped all around it from every side and every angle, along with hot pink and purple bougainvillea covering its entranceway like a soft blanket.

Leila and Faye fly over. They're holding a tray in the middle of them with three saucers, cups, a tea kettle, and a plate of steaming, fluffy croissants. They place the tea cups that resemble white lilies down. In a white ceramic bowl next to us are lemons. Then a jar of honey is placed next to the lemons. Little white delicate spoons shaped like lily pads are placed inside each of the cups. It's a superb matching set, placed there perfectly to go along with everything else that's perfect in this world—at least that's what it seems like to me. *Yup. Complete perfection.*

Leila pours the hot tea in the queen's cup first, then proceeds to pour mine, while Faye pours some tea for Noah.

Taking her long, delicate sip, "Mmmm. Delicious," the queen says.

I copy along with Noah. My eyes rotate from fairy to fairy, peeking above my tea cup, and then setting it back down on the table. "Yes, it is. Thank you."

The yummy croissants are releasing a delicious, steamy, buttery scent. My stomach rumbles, wondering if it's too early to pick one up. *Would it be totally rude if I just grab it? I'm starving!*

"Thank you, my queen." Noah repeats.

Leave it to Noah to have such manners. I have to casually roll my eyes for a moment, because there's nothing this boy doesn't do right. But, it's more contagious than annoying—he makes you want to be a better person around him.

"Seraphina," the queen announces. "We must talk about your journey today, and get you prepared, because it's time for you to go soon."

I take another sip of tea, and cough as it goes down the wrong pipe. "Ahem," I cough again louder. "Sorry, excuse me." My eyes scan the queen. "Yes, I understand. So, what is it that I have to do?" I bite my cuticles.

"First, why don't you eat a little something? Instead of your fingers." The queen's eyes go from my hand in my mouth to the plate of steaming croissants on the table. "You must be starved."

"Oh, yeah." I don't hesitate, snatching one up.

Queen Ivy turns around to say something to Leila and Faye. "Ladies, please bring us the map of Raiven right away. Thank you."

Both fairies scatter away at their queen's pressing request.

Two minutes later, they fly back with the map and drop it in front of us. Noah sits to the side, listening and observing her every word.

I'm inhaling my croissant, which I can't chew quick enough; I'm so hungry.

"So, you will leave my castle here," she places her finger down on the castle on the map. "And travel through this invisible door to the west," tracing her finger along the arrow, going to the left direction on the map. "Again, you will see and go through this door only with the help of the pixie dust, which I have already given to Noah."

She glances over at Noah who's sitting there patiently, of course. "Noah?"

"Yes, my queen. It's safe in here with me." He pats a pouch that is tied around his petite waistline.

"Can I have it please, Noah?" Queen Ivy requests sticking out her hand, palm up.

"Yes, my queen," Noah responds. He unties this small pouch from around this rope that holds it around his waist, putting the pouch in the queen's flower-like hand.

"Thank you, Noah."

Noah nods.

The queen opens up the pouch and takes a tiny pinch of pixie dust between her thumb and index finger, sprinkling it in my tea. "Here. Drink up. This is going to give you a boost to send you on your way. It will wear off, so it's up to Noah to give you the rest throughout your journey, to his discretion of course."

"Yes, my queen," he nods, appeasing her.

I look at the queen then at Noah, hesitating. Noah gives me the gesture of a quick nod of his head to let me know that it's fine.

I pick up the tea cup and take another sip. "Ok, if you say so."

"Now, in about five minutes you will start feeling impeccable and unstoppable, physically stronger, with even keener senses. You will feel like you can fly—absolutely weightless." Queen Ivy lifts up her arms, embracing the air effortlessly.

I remember my dream from last night. If it makes me feel anything like that, I can be sure I'm going to love this pixie dust stuff.

"And last but not least, you will have visions of your friend, Josie Lee. So, don't be startled. She is already with you all the time. You just can't always see her. The pixie dust helps open up a channel, so you can see her. She will also be your guide through this. So, there is nothing to fear, but fear itself. Remember, Seraphina, it's all in here." Queen Ivy brushes her three soft fingers against the temples of my face; they move down slowly to my cheek, giving me the chills as they travel.

I close my eyes, and then open them, staring into Queen Ivy's hazel ones. It hits me—the pixie dust. I feel it, tinkling all over my body. Weightless is definitely the best word to describe the sensation. Taking a deep inhalation, my sinuses open up; I can even breathe better. My ears pop slightly. Background noises that were a few minutes ago far away are now coming from right behind my head. I can sense all the tastes in the air, prickling around in my mouth.

The feeling is sensational. I feel like I just dove into a warm, aqua-blue ocean. I've never ever felt anything so carefree before. Except, however, for maybe one thing; the way I felt when I was with my best friend, Josie Lee.

Then, it dawns on me. *Josie Lee? Goodness Gracious!* I realize what the queen just said; that I will get to see her again. Just as the idea passes in my mind, there she is in front of me, glimmering like a gem and dazzling in the sunlight, so peaceful. Just like that day in the hopsital room. In that same, glittering gown. All of the hairs plunk up on my entire body. Rubbing my eyes, I can't believe it's really her, and she's such a wondrous vision

CHAPTER TWELVE

My Very Own Unicorn

"JOSIE LEE...JOSIE LEE?" I cry out, throwing my arms up in the air, jumping up from my seat, and running over to the transparent shape. But, just as I get there, Josie Lee is gone. The only thing left behind is a faded smile. Josie Lee's smile is now the only thing imprinted on my brain—no touch, no shape, no body; gone, gone, gone.

"Josie Lee...no...why? Why did you leave me again?" I choke up.

Queen Ivy and Noah come over to me. "My sweet, sweet, darling," Queen Ivy tucks my loose strand of hair behind my ear. "She is not gone, but forever here by your side indeed." This reminds me of my mom. I *sniffle* and glance back at both fairies.

"It's true, Seraphina," Noah confirms. "She is, and you will see her again. When the time is right, and you're ready for it. Just have faith."

"But why couldn't she just stay now? I don't understand." The tears start falling; I wipe them from my wet cheeks.

"She was just giving you a glimpse to let you know she'll be with you. But, your frequency level has not been raised enough yet. You haven't been here long enough," Noah clarifies. "In time, you will see."

"I will?" *Sniff, sniff.*

"Yes, you will." Queen Ivy confirms. "Now, we must be on our way."

∿

IT MUST BE SOMEWHERE in the middle of the afternoon; one, two o'clock? I'm not sure.

Noah is preparing himself; he ties the pixie dust pouch back around his waist and tightens a belt-like strap around one of his shoulders, which hoists a bow and arrows. *What will he need that for?* I know the answer, but really don't want to know.

I bite at one of my cuticles, trying not to think about what scary evil lies ahead. Right now, I'm wishing I were back at home, even though South Florida hasn't even been my home for that long. To me, home is where my family is, and Raiven is not that place—even with all its beauty and kind creatures.

I can still feel the effects of the pixie dust—light and fluffy—ready to take on the world — literally. Gazing down at my T-shirt that says LOVE with blue, white, and sparkly, silver colors splattered around it, my skinny, ripped jeans, shoeless feet, and my black and white low-top sneakers in hand, I can't help but think to myself that this is the outfit I'm going to do it in. *Funny.*

"Seraphina," Noah interrupts my self-musing—something he's good at. "Are you ready?"

"As ready as I'll ever be." I throw my hands up in the air as if surrendering to what will be.

"Before you go, I want you to meet someone." Just at that moment, I'm startled by Queen Ivy walking up behind us with a snow-white horse, with a long, rainbow-colored mane and tail. A sharp, sparkly, pointy horn rests on its nose. It is also multicolored like a rainbow, which matches its beautiful hair.

With grace, it follows just to the side of the queen as she leads it unleashed, but seemingly tamed.

"Goodness Gracious" I blurt out. "That is one gorgeous horse." My mouth dangles open.

The queen chuckles and throws her head back. "Why, don't you dare offend her like that again. She is no horse. She is your *unicorn*. Horses have no magical powers."

I grovel. "Oh, sorry."

"Unicorns are a whole other story. Magical beyond measure. And you, Seraphina, birthed her when you wished upon a shooting star." Queen Ivy pats the unicorn's side.

The unicorn bobbles her head up and down. She makes a horse noise or unicorn noise—whatever that is—almost like she's greeting me. *Neigh...neigh!*

"Can I pet her?" I reach out my hand.

"Well, of course you can. She belongs to you." Queen Ivy gestures for me to come toward the unicorn, inviting me to pet her.

I glide over and raise my hand to the unicorn. She positions her head down, so I can touch the top of her nose. Her fur is soft like silk, and her horn glitters with every color of the rainbow. The unicorn's eyes are emerald green. "She's...she's...stunning!" I can barely make out the words.

"Yes, she is." Noah agrees, adjusting his gear around his small frame, staring at the unicorn as well. "It's not every day here we see unicorns. They come around only under special circumstances. And this, well, this is definitely one of them. Great job, Seraphina. She was created based on your imagination. You've got a great one."

"But, how? I don't understand. I don't remember ever thinking about a unicorn."

Noah adds. "The universe knows and matches what's in your heart. Somewhere in your life, you thought her up. Maybe in your subconscious. You just didn't realize it."

"Well," Queen Ivy wonders, "What are you going to name her?"

"Name her? You want me to name her?"

"She is your unicorn, silly, so it's only appropriate that you find a well-suited name for her."

A brief moment passes, and I'm brainstorming on a name. And it just hits me; out of thin air. "She was birthed from a star, so I think I'll call her Stella."

There was a girl in my class back in New Jersey whose name was Stella. I remember her sharing with the class on the first day of school, when we had to introduce ourselves, that her name means to be a star and she believed that she'd be famous one day.

The queen lights up. "Sounds perfect."

"Yeah. Perfect, right?" I ask while petting and admiring my new, beautiful unicorn. "Wow, I can't believe I actually have a real-live unicorn."

Stella bobbles her head and *neighs* again, gesturing that she agrees it's quite perfect.

I stop petting Stella for a moment and look at the queen. "When you said that unicorns have magical powers, what did you mean exactly?" I ask as I pick at one of my cuticles.

The queen shoots me that look.

"Oh, sorry." I fling my finger from my mouth.

"Well," Queen Ivy sighs, "she can read your mind and feel all of your emotions. So, don't be surprised if Stella is in total synch with you at all times. You can ride her anytime you like, especially when you're tired. But, the most significant thing about her is her horn. Inside of it contains a magical dust, which if consumed, can completely heal you. Plus, it's connected to Raiven and Raiven to her horn. The magic all resides within both in complete harmony. Her power only works here, so she would not survive in another realm on planet Earth. But also, most importantly, her horn is powerful enough that if it's cut or taken from her, she can die."

I gasp. "Oh, no!"

"And that's not the worst of it. In order for Witch Alyssa to gain complete control over Raiven, she must sacrifice a unicorn and offer its horn to her evil god to please. So, we mustn't let that wicked woman get her hands on Stella."

Queen Ivy pets Stella, gazing at her innocence and beauty.

"But, how do I do that?" I ask with a shaky voice.

"Stella is pretty strong. She can handle herself for the most part. However, you both still must guard and protect each other, along with Noah, of course. He's here to help at all costs." The queen winks at her little warrior fairy; he returns the motion.

I dangle my head down and wave it from side to side; I want to cry. "I can't...I can't...do this..."

"Now, now, child." Queen Ivy takes her two soft fingers to lift my chin up.

Noah strokes my back, and Stella thrusts her head up and down.

"The three of you—" the queen points to Noah, then Stella, and then me "—now all have one another. You will be safe. Noah is very good at what he does." She winks again in his direction. "Between him and Stella, they will ward off anything harmful that comes your way. Also, don't forget Josie Lee will be a guide to you as well."

I express a subtle smile, feeling better knowing that I'm not alone. *Plus, what kid my age has a warrior fairy and unicorn?*

Aha. Actually, I don't think there is any human in the world who does.

"Remember something. The power is all in here." Queen Ivy taps me on my forehead. "You can accomplish anything you set your mind to. You just have to believe in yourself." She is now holding my face in her hands and staring into my eyes.

A couple tears roll down my cheeks. My face scrunches up, and I nod my head. *Maybe I can do this after all?*

Queen Ivy plants a tiny kiss on my forehead. "Come now, let's walk to the first invisible door. I will take you there. But then the rest is up to you." She strides in the other direction. Noah, Stella, and I all follow behind her.

CHAPTER THIRTEEN

The Red, Evil Realm

IN FRONT of my eyes are two, rocky cliffs with green moss growing all over them. In between these magnificent cliffs is a massive, strong, flowing waterfall with a rainbow—running from one end to the other—glowing in front of it. It pours down to a river, which turns and ends into a small, circular stream, about the size of a football field.

The light, misty breeze blows across my face from the wind, which carries the water with it.

Queen Ivy inhales deeply then turns to face me. "Now, is the time I must tell you the plan on how to get back the rainbow crystal. But, first...Noah?"

"Yes, my queen," he answers swiftly at her request. Even his little body frame jumps when she calls him.

"Please do it now," she commands.

"Yes, my queen." He reaches inside his pouch and pulls out a small handful of pixie dust. He thrusts it in the air, and the breeze carries it away. The pixie dust swirls in mid-air, trailing around before it ends up looking like a funnel. It swirls and swirls until an iridescent door appears, which floats in mid-air. As the pixie dust takes on more of a substance, it transforms the door from an iridescent form into an actual white door with a solid, gold knob. It sits just about at my waistline, reaching the height of Noah.

I giggle and put my hand over my mouth. I've been to circuses and seen magic shows, but I've never seen anything like this before.

Noah looks at me with his head somewhat cocked to the side. "What is it?" He asks me.

I release my hand from my mouth. "I have to say...that was actually pretty flippin' awesome!"

"Yeah. I guess you're right." He examines the door. "It is cool. There's a lot of magic that occurs in our world, Seraphina. So, better start getting used to it now."

Noah walks over to the door and grabs the knob. He turns it slowly, and it creaks open. The open door is now floating in mid-air. "After you." Opening up his arms, he signals for me to go in and walk through.

I look at the queen for her last and final words before my long journey ahead. She turns to me and squeezes me one last time. My feet sink into the cool grass below.

"When you cross through this door, Seraphina, you will be entering the red, evil realm of our world. No one ever goes there, except the sinful. You are to go and get back the crystal from the treacherous witch." The queen's body quivers. "You will be carefully looked after." She nods at Noah and Stella, and then takes a deep breath. "I believe it's within you. You can do this. Her castle exists at the northwest side of this realm."

I can't help but think, *no one goes there, except for me. Sure.*

Queen Ivy opens up my hand with hers. "Here is a pocket compass to help you find your way." In it, she places a glass pocket compass with a gold chain attached then folds my hand closed. "Don't lose this or you'll get lost."

The breeze of water mist is splashing my face.

I inhale deeply as if my life depends on this one breath. Noah is still standing there, holding the door open, while Stella waits patiently beside us.

The queen continues. "When you enter the witch's realm, you must find her castle in the pits of a muddy, foggy, grey underworld. You'll have to cross the bridge, through and over the moat, but you must sneak inside. Her trolls remain on guard, yet they are some of the heaviest sleepers, so this must be done late at night while they are snoring away."

Standing there next to an open, floating door, I squeeze the compass tighter in my hand, and shut my eyes for a brief moment, bracing myself in my mind on what that place could possibly be like. I tremble.

"When you get into the witch's castle, you will have to find where she is holding the crystal," she explains.

Opening my eyes, I stutter with fear. "But—but how am I going to get away with getting the crystal back from her? She'll ca-catch me and ki-kill me."

The queen shakes her head. "Not if she's not there to see you. You must go when she is away from the crystal. She is known to hold a nightly ritual where she talks to and pleases her evil god. She must have some sort of an altar in her castle where she does this. You must wait for her to be doing so—where she is distant and at her most vulnerable."

"I will guide you through it." Noah gently places his hand on my lower back.

How can a little, three-foot fairy possibly help me, let alone save my life, if I were to need it? It's a strange thought. But, I don't want to say that out loud and hurt his feelings, so I just nod my head. Noah only means well, and I do really like him.

He is one of the sweetest people—or fairies rather—I've ever known. That really does sound so silly when I say that to myself. *A fairy? Come on, really?* Sometimes, I still have to pinch myself to make sure this isn't all just some wacked-out, crazy dream.

"Seraphina? Are you still with us?" Queen Ivy waves her hand in front of my face.

"Oh, yes, of course. I'm sorry." I shake my head.

"Ok, then." She proceeds. "Once you get back the rainbow crystal...again, *hopefully*..."

"Yes, '*hopefully*,'" I add.

"... then—just to reiterate—you will go on to the orange realm (land of gigantic honey bees), through to the yellow realm (land of sunshine and sunflowers), into the green realm (crystal forest of the elves), then up to the blue (water realm), and lastly to the violet realm, returning the rainbow crystal to Wizard Arbit Maximus, who is patiently waiting to see you with the crystal, of course."

"Of course." I add with an insecure smile.

"It's ok, Seraphina. We'll do it—together—me, you, and Stella." Noah pats me on the arm. He always has a way to make me feel better.

Stella neighs and trembles her head to let me know that she is with me on this as well.

"And that's that," Queen Ivy finalizes. Turning to face Noah, she reaches out to hand him the map of Raiven. "And you mustn't forget this. Put it in a safe place." She smiles in Noah's direction.

"Of course I will, my queen." Noah puts the map in a satchel, which is strapped around his torso, along with his bow and arrows. "It is safe here with me." He bows to his queen.

The queen caresses his head. "There is no better warrior

fairy in all our land that could guard and protect Seraphina the way that you can."

He stands back up to face her. "Thank you, my queen. I will guard her with my life."

Noah shifts his body toward me and points to my feet. "I suggest you put those shoes on now. You will need them once we cross. It's a whole different realm over there."

I throw my sneakers down on the ground and then slip them back on, one by one. Afterward, I pause, looking through the floating open door. "Here goes nothing." I take a deep breath and climb through.

SWOOSH... *swoosh... swoosh.* At a rapid speed, I am sliding through a funnel of some sort—or at least, that's what it feels like to me — like I'm going down a huge slide. I whip my head back to get a glimpse of Noah and Stella, sliding behind me. Noah's facial expression is ordinary; he doesn't look scared or excited. *How does he do that? I'm screaming inside! Where are we going?* Just may be to an eternal hellfire pit for all I know.

The screaming starts on the inside. Yet somehow it just slips out of my mouth, "Arghhh!"

Noah yells back from behind me, "Hold on. I'm right behind you."

I hear a couple of *neighs* coming from Stella, sounding like she's in distress. Probably is, if she feels what I feel.

All of a sudden, the slide ends, and we are lead out of an opening (the invisible, floating door) that leads to another realm, and not a very nice-looking one. The three of us land smack in mucky, soggy mud. I'm thrown onto my behind. "Ouch!" I lean to one side and rub it.

Noah bounces on his feet without falling, yet he splashes

mud onto my face. Wiping it off, I grant him a sarcastic smile. "Oh, gee, thanks."

Stella lands with her front legs bent, and her butt in the air. She makes a loud exhale through her nose. Her nostrils flare and jiggle. *Puff. Puff.*

"Sorry, my dear lady," Noah replies. He extends his arm to me to help me up out of the mud.

There's nothing around us other than miles of this soggy, muddy mess. It's a swamp with big, ugly, croaking toads in all directions. Reminds me of the Everglades in Florida, and it feels just like that—except darker, drearier, and much more gross. There isn't an ounce of sunshine. The sky looks completely grey. Some of the mud is bubbling.

"Oh good grief! How are we going to get through this?" I ask.

"We will ride together on Stella's back. She will take us through it," Noah replies.

Stella nods her head and sits her butt down, so we can jump on-top. Noah gestures for me to get on first, and then he climbs on behind me. He clamps his hands onto the back of my shirt, holding on. Stella gets up and takes her first step, struggling a bit.

"Wait." Noah exclaims. "I must sprinkle some pixie dust first." He takes a pinch of it out of his pouch around his waist then thrusts it in the air. An invisible door appears—the one that we just flew out of. "Read your compass, so we can remember our exact location to get back out of this place after we've gotten the crystal. This realm is the only one with no rainbow or water-fall to mark its spot. We mustn't forget – it's our only way out."

I snatch the compass out of my pocket and read its location aloud. "We're at one-hundred and eighty-two degrees south." I situate the compass back in my pocket. "Do you know the way to the witch's castle?"

"The map." He takes it out of his satchel and opens it up and views the witch's castle marked in the red realm. "Here." Noah points to it on the map. "We have to go west," then gestures to our right. "It's in that direction."

And so we begin venturing that way, step by step; Stella, drudging through the mud, passing hundreds of croaking toads with disgusting warts. *Croak...croak...croak!*

Gross.

CHAPTER FOURTEEN

Through the Marsh and Moat

WE STUMBLE upon a large body of water with some type of green film covering it. It has green lily pads, sprouting up everywhere. Due to the film being so thick and a cloud of fog that hovers over, I can't see what lurks beneath. There's a broken-down, wooden sign in front of the pond. I read the sign out loud, "'Belief Bog—Down through the marsh and out through the fog, only belief will build a bridge, and up will pop a log.'"

"Shoot. What does that mean?" I ask Noah.

Noah pats the side of Stella. She kneels for him to get off. He walks over to the sign and reads it, rubbing his chin. "Hmm?"

While Noah is trying to figure it out, I realize there is no way to pass this body of water without literally crossing over it. *But how?* It stretches for miles in every direction. I remember some of the poetry I've studied in school. *Maybe it's some sort of a riddle?*

I smack at my arms and legs; mosquitoes are biting me

everywhere. I notice an unusually big one on the side of my arm; I slap it dead and blood splatters. "Ekkk!" I rub the blood off on my pants. Then I witness gigantic cockroaches, crawling in around us all over the ground. And flies are swarming around our heads. "Good grief! We have to get out of here fast. This place is infested with the most disgusting insects ever."

"Aha. I think I get it," Noah says. "I think what it's trying to say is that if somehow we just believe in its presence, even though we can't see it...in the marsh, under all that fog, a log will pop up for us, using it to cross over as a bridge. You know? To carry us to the other side." He points in the endless direction of nowhere.

"Wow. Pretty impressive. You got it just like that, huh?" I snap my fingers stunned.

"It sounds right, though, doesn't it?" His hands rest on his hips.

"Actually,it does."

Even Stella bobbles her head up and down.

"Well, thank you." Noah bows.

Noah jumps back on Stella; she takes a step closer to the marsh.

"But, how do we do it? How do we believe?" I ask.

"It's something you can do from your heart. It has to come from within. Close your eyes and feel it. See the log popping up —believe it, and you will receive it," Noah responds.

I shut my eyes, take a deep breath, and I envision a big log popping up, floating above in the marsh. Then, I open my eyes back up. "Believe, believe. I don't know, Noah."

"No, don't doubt. Just believe. Breathe through it. Take a leap of faith."

Taking a few more breaths, I stall, staring at the scary water. "Ok, Stella, go."

Stella hesitates and then takes a slow step into the marsh.

But, nothing appears. She falls, dangling half in the water and half out; almost falling completely in.

I scream. "Arghhh! Nooooo!" We both dangle from Stella, holding on for dear life. Noah's off to the side trying to hang on; half of his body emerged in the mucky water. He clamps down on my shirt even harder.

Two heads with rotating eyeballs bobble up through the marsh and gradually begin swimming closer to us.

"What...what...are those?" I'm shaking uncontrollably.

Noah glances down. "Don't look. They're crocodiles. And they're waiting for us to fall in to eat us. So, please, Seraphina, try again. You have to save us. We can't hold on much longer. I'd fly but my wings are wet, and I can't. So you just have to believe."

I close my eyes tighter this time. "Ok, Seraphina—" And as soon as I say my own name I feel a slight breeze through my hair and hear a soft whisper in my ear. "You can do it, Seraphina. The log is there. Just look."

Holy Mackerel! It's Josie Lee's voice. I can hear her, clear as day. I open my eyes, and the water begins bubbling, like something is trying to push its way to the top. *Bloop...bloop...bloop.*

"That's it. That's it, Seraphina. You're doing it! It's working." Noah shouts.

In an instant, I don't question its existence any longer. It's there; the log, the bridge to carry us through to the other side. It pops up out of the water and stops Stella from falling in any deeper.

I sit up straight and grab Noah, bolstering him back upright onto my unicorn's back, sighing. Noah pats my back. "Good job. I knew you could do it."

"Thanks," I say, "but I thought you were supposed to be the warrior. Phew." I wipe the sweat from my forehead. "That was a close call."

NIGHT TIME APPROACHES; I yawn on Stella's back. My eyes keep closing on and off, but I'm doing everything to keep them open. Walking through the trenches of torture is enough to keep anyone awake.

Feeling sluggish as well, I can also feel Stella's steps become slower and slower.

Two, big, black vultures follow in close proximity behind us, and loud toads croak throughout the eerie night-air. A couple of black crows are flying up in the sky, circling our heads. Everything about this place makes the tiny hairs on my arms stand up, and not in a good way.

"When do we get there?" I ask Noah groggily. "I'm so sleepy. I need a rest."

"Very soon," he responds. "According to the map, we are probably just about five or six miles away from Witch Alyssa's castle. It will be the perfect time to arrive because her trolls should be asleep, and when trolls sleep, they sleep hard. I will give you some pixie dust when we arrive. It will wake you right up."

Stella makes a loud *neigh* at Noah.

"It's ok, girl." He pats Stella's side.

"What's wrong with her?" I ask. *I should know.*

"Everything you feel, she feels, remember? She feels your energy depleted, so hers is as well. When the pixie dust lifts your spirits, hers will rise to meet you." Noah grins.

I GAZE up at the pitch-black sky to get a glimpse of a full, yellow-white moon. It's our only light at this point. We finally stop at a castle and moat. Even the castle looks evil. It has no color and sharp edges (like it was carved out of some dead tree bark), and heavy fog shields it. The bright moon stands out from behind the castle, just enough for us to get a view of the spooky sight.

A chill, running up and down my spine makes me tremble. "I-is...th-that...where I have to go in to get the rainbow crystal?" I point a shaky hand in the direction of the castle.

"Sorry to say this, but, yes." Noah taps the back of my shoulder.

"H-how?" I swallow hard.

Noah pats Stella's side again. "Let me down, girl, please."

Stella does as she's asked. Noah leaps down and gestures for me to get down as well.

He reaches back into his satchel and pulls out the pixie dust. "Close your eyes."

I inhale deeply with my eyes shut. Noah sprinkles the pixie dust over my head.

In a matter of five seconds, I already start feeling better. That warm and tingly sensation pierces throughout my body, feeling like I can conquer the world.

"Remember, never doubt yourself. Just like you did back there at the marsh. You can do it. You must believe in yourself."

I look at Noah and nod. My body is tingling everywhere, and I feel weightless. "Ok. I'm ready."

"I will be right there with you in case any of the trolls should wake. I have my bow and arrows right here." He taps it as it hangs around his shoulder. "Stella will be out here waiting for our return. She now has the energy to ride like the wind and carry us back out of here when we have the crystal."

Stella nods her head—this time with more energy.

"Ok, let's go. You first." He puts his arm out in front of me to lead the way.

"Me first?" I poke myself.

"Well, you are the chosen one, aren't you? And a lady, might I add." He grins. I am a gentleman.

"Sure. Thanks a lot." I roll my eyes, taking the first step, then the second – leading the way up to the bridge, past the moat, and right in front of the evil witch's castle.

"Here goes nothing." I take one last deep breath and look around. "Oh goodness. How are we going to get inside?"

"Well, we obviously can't walk in through the front without being noticed, even if her trolls are in there asleep. We can't risk it." Noah points to a window with a murky, white film over it. It has a crack in the glass. "We'll climb through there."

While walking side by side over to the window, Noah takes a cloth out from inside his satchel. He wraps it around his fist and punches open the crack even larger—large enough for both of us to climb in. Fortunately, the sound isn't too loud or alarming.

"This time, I'll go first," he tells me.

"Great. Why thank you." I say with sarcasm.

Noah climbs in, and then I hear a little thump from the outside. "You ok?" I ask him almost at a whisper, holding in a chuckle.

"Yeah, but it's just a bit of a steep fall when you come in, so be careful."

As I try and scramble through it, I get a flashback of the night Josie Lee and I were climbing out of her window to sneak out. At that moment, I stall and my stomach aches; I wish Josie Lee was here with me. And with that thought, somebody or something almost pushes me hard enough to make me fly through the window to the inside. As if I were kicked right in the butt. *Ha. Ha. Very funny. I have a hint of what or who, rather, it could've been. Uh-huh.*

CHAPTER FIFTEEN

An Evil Witch and Her Trolls

I LAND with a hard thump on the cold floor. A cloud of dust forms around my face, and I cough. *Whoa.* No one has been in this room for a long time.

I stand up and examine the room. Noah is already up and roaming around it. I see him staring at what looks like a dusty crystal ball. There's a big, black book lying on a broken-down desk next to where I landed. I wipe off a layer of dust to see what it says. It reads *Witchcraft.* The letters are in red, gothic font. A fake spider with red, matching, twinkling eyes dangles next to the *Witchcraft* letters. Wanting nothing to do with it, I throw it across the room.

The noise startles Noah; he jumps and then turns to look at me. "Shhh!" His index finger covers his lips. "What would you do that for? Are you trying to wake those cruel critters?"

"Sorry. It's just that that book freaked me out." It's now lying in the corner of the room on the floor. Above it, in the ceiling, is a real spider web—half broken on one end and dangling. Even the spider has moved on to another location. The room looks like no one has been in there for ages. An ancient chandelier hangs in the middle of the ceiling, but doesn't work. All the bulbs in it are cracked; one even fell out and shattered glass on the floor.

I step on a piece of broken glass at one point and hear a loud *crunch.* "Noah, careful."

"Oh, I'll be ok. These things?" He points to his bare feet. "They're made out of rubber. But, see now, why I told you to wear your shoes here? Not like back at Fairyland."

There's that teacher-like lecturing way about him that sneaks in from time to time. "I get it, thanks." I smile with a closed mouth. "What now?"

"We should just keep on moving." He walks over to a door in the room, which is shut, and opens it slowly. "Just stay close to me, and quiet."

"Where do you think she keeps it?" I whisper close to his ear while following him out the door into the castle.

We enter a long corridor of some sort with multiple accesses to different rooms. The corridor leads to another open room with a spiral staircase, smack in the middle of it. It's got paintings on the walls of what looks like other witches; maybe they're powerful ones that came before her that the witch admires or something.

The old, wooden floors creak as we walk. Small step by small step, I'm following behind Noah's little frame, but huge, glittering wings. Between the witchcraft book and spiders, creaky floors, and weird paintings of witches, I'm shuddering inside – feels more like convulsions at this point. "I—I'm scared, Noah. How are we going to get away with this?" I ask with a soft, trembling voice.

"Not sure yet," he whispers. "But, we'll figure something out. First, we have to find where exactly in this castle are Witch

Alyssa and her trolls so we can cover our tracks, then go find the crystal." Noah slithers across the floor, carefully looking over each of his shoulders and grasping onto his bow and arrows.

Suddenly, we hear loud noises and talking coming from the top of the tower, above the staircase. He points at it. "Let's go check it out."

We both grab onto the wooden railing. It's hard and strong; it feels unbreakable to me. This all seems too big for me to undertake—this huge castle and powerful witch. *This is crazy.*

We creep up one stair at a time, trying not to make the slightest noise. A downpour of rain resonates, coming from outside, beating down on the massive glass windows throughout the castle. One of the step creaks, and Noah stops dead in his tracks, throwing his arm out to the side. I take that as a sign to stop as well. A few seconds pass. Nothing. So, we keep going. We finally reach the top of the tower. There's a door, but it is cracked open just a bit with a band of light coming through.

Noah gestures behind him—without turning around—for me to get down low to the ground. Gazing through the small opening of the door, I see her. Witch Alyssa.

Wicked, crystal blue eyes highlighted with thick, black eyeliner peer from inside a crystal ball. Two hands clasp it with long, black, pointy fingernails. She is wearing a blood-red corset, laced-up dress, and black cloak. The hood of the cloak fits her head like a glove, while a jeweled headband peeks out. A black stone rests in the middle of her forehead. Her milky-white skin and blue eyes seem to glow.

Witch Alyssa turns from the crystal ball to walk over to a rickety-looking wooden stand. It holds a beaming, multi-colored crystal the shape of an enormous diamond, but about the size of a soccer ball. It's assembled inside of this stand at a perfect, upright position. It's held together by a hole in the middle, which was drilled exactly to the shape of the crystal to steady it in its place.

The hairs on my body rise just from the sight of it. "Wow," I whisper.

Alyssa picks up the crystal and admires its beauty. Immediately, all the blotches, veins, and age marks on her hands and arms disappear. The skin on her face becomes younger and healthier looking. Her skin glows like a golden tan after a long day at the beach. The red line around her lips starts to become darker then fills the rest of her lips, coloring them in fuller and even redder. Crystal, clear, blue-white eyes twinkle under her hood, losing any redness or puffiness to them. Her red hair goes from limp, broken and damaged to luscious plumps of curls, glistening and shining like how it would on a hair commercial.

She walks over to a full-length, gothic mirror, hanging on her wall and views her newer, younger-looking self. "Yes, yes." The witch cackles and tosses her head back. "Aren't I perfect?" she asks two of the ugliest-looking creatures.

Well, guess they're not asleep. Just great.

Their skin tone is greenish/grayish with craters on their faces. Their noses make up more of a shape of widened golf balls than they do of actual noses. In response to their witch's remark, they make grunting noises in agreement, drooling out of the sides of their mouths.

"Well, speak up, idiots!" Her full, red lips pout.

"Yes...yes...madam," one squeaks out with a treacherous mouth.

"Yes what?" The witch now has her pointy fingernails wrapped around her waistline, where her long hair reaches.

"Yes, you're beautiful?" The troll with out-of-control, frizzy, black hair asks, not knowing which the proper response is.

"Oh, shut up!" The witch leans down and smacks him on the side of the head. "I said, perfect. Get it right, stupid!"

He hunches his small three-foot body over like a scared, scrawny dog. "So sorry to upset you, madam." His voice quivers.

Alyssa sighs and pulls back the hood off of her head. "Fine. Just don't let it happen again."

Both of the trolls stare at her beauty, drooling and grunting with even more admiration and obsession.

The other ugly troll says, "Why, madam, you are simply exquisite." His sharp teeth overlap his slobbering, bottom lip.

She examines her ageless hands, smiling from ear to ear. "I know." She looks down at her two, creature companions. "But in order to keep it, not go back to my old withering age, and to live forever, we have to now sacrifice the unicorn to please our evil god." Her eyes squint with pleasure.

Both trolls giggle, which sound like little children who enjoy doing something bad.

"First, we'll have to get rid of that annoying, little, smelly fairy. Get that pest out of our way. Kidnap the girl—and her unicorn—then bring them to me."

"What about the great and powerful Wizard Arbit Maximus?" The other troll with grey, frizzy hair asks in a raspy, nasal-like voice.

Alyssa throws him an evil eye, which twinkles in his direction. "Don't you dare try and proclaim that there is one more powerful than me. I have the crystal now. Once the unicorn is sacrificed, it's mine—all mine. And there is nothing he can do."

"Sorry, madam. You're right, none more powerful than you." The troll agrees. He hunches over, twiddling his distorted fingers together.

"Even get rid of that Ivy. That *stupid* fairy they call their Queen. That's not a queen. I'm a queen and will eventually rule over all the realms in Raiven. And you two? My little princes." She smirks maliciously. "And you and your fellow trolls will rule over all of Fairyland, and you can eat those smelly twerps for breakfast." Witch Alyssa rubs the bottom of their bumpy chins as they sneer and delight at the thought.

She walks across the room over to a cage filled with bats, which are flapping their rubbery wings, and grabs one. "In the meantime, I must continue to please my god." Alyssa takes the frenzied bat and places it on a bloody table. A black, fuzzy spider scurries across it, passing her hand. Next to the bat lies a long, thin needle. She picks it up and stares at it with penetrating eyes, and then slides it into the bat's heart, killing the poor thing.

I shudder. Even though those things freak me out, I still feel bad. The spider scurries beneath the table.

Her arms are raised to the sky to praise and please her evil god. The bright, red blood now drips down both of her arms. She begins speaking loud and intensely, in some sort of language I've never heard before. As the witch holds her arms up high, I hear a large *strike* of lightning, followed by *rumbling* thunder.

I feel like I might faint. *Get me outta here!* As I go to turn around and run in the other direction, Noah grabs onto my leg and stops me. "Where are you going? You can't give up now. We've made it this far already."

"Noah, I can't. I just can't." I yell, but at a whisper. "I'm not...I'm not the chosen one. You guys are just confused. You've got the wrong person." I bite, ripping off one of my cuticles off my finger. "I'm just a young, average girl from New Jersey. I can't even watch scary movies or handle a spirit-talking board game. How am I going to save Raiven? And...and...this lady is flippin' psycho!" I take just enough of a break between sentences to chew more fingers; one even bleeds. *Enough blood for one night, please.* I squint; my eyes almost shut.

Noah is crouched down low to the ground, looking at me. His stare goes deep into my soul. "Seraphina, you are only as good or powerful as you tell yourself. The only limits we place on ourselves are the barriers we create in our own minds. But really there are no such things—they actually don't exist. They only exist because we tell ourselves that they do." Then, he lets go of me. "But go if you must. Nobody is forcing you to stay. Ultimately, it's your choice." He turns back around, looking at Alyssa who is now pouring the bat blood into a wine glass.

I'm frozen there in time and space for a moment, but it feels like eternity. I never really thought about it like that since I've been in this new world. *My choice?* No one ever told me that I had to do it. It's not like anyone put a gun to my head. *But why? Why have I chosen to stay all this time so far in Raiven—far away from my family and home? To see Josie Lee?* But, I haven't even seen her other than for a brief moment. *And will I see her again? Who knows? But why me?* And then deep down inside, I can feel it; like a calling—like someone or something is compelling me to do it—to stay. *Maybe it is Josie Lee? Not sure.* But it's almost like I can feel a connection; with me to Raiven, and Raiven to Earth. It's all linked together like a perfect triangle. I have been chosen by some force. I stare at the back of Noah's head, lost in thought. And then it dawns on me. *Well, why not me? Plus, someone needs to stop this psycho. Kidnap me and hurt Stella? No way! I can't give up now; I've made it this far.*

"Ok, I'll do it," I shout. I jump up and land with a loud *thump* on both of my feet with my arms crossed.

Witch Alyssa is about to drink from the glass, but stops in her tracks. She twists and faces the opening of the door. "Who's there?"

"Quick." Noah points for me to hide behind a gigantic vase with black roses in it, while he hides in a small closet next to the room. I do as I'm told. Behind a vase isn't exactly the best hiding spot, but I'm too nervous to think up my own plan and really don't have other options at the moment.

I can hear Witch Alyssa walk over to the opening and put

her hand on the door until it creaks open even more. She's sniffing the air. *Whiff, whiff.* "Hmmm? Smells too pretty here for my liking." She turns back around to call on her trolls. "Boys?"

I'm quivering so bad I have to hug my own body at this point. My heart is pounding out of my chest. *Please don't find me, please don't find me.*

"Yes, madam," they both say.

The witch's footsteps *clatter* as she walks back into the room to address the ugly critters. "Search the premises. There must be a fairy nearby. I can smell it. Eeek!"

I poke my head out from behind the vase to get a glimpse of Noah doing the same from inside the closet. He gestures for me to run back down the stairs. He whispers. "Now. Go. Now is our chance."

Without hesitation, I run as fast as my legs can carry me. Down the stairs, through the corridor, and back into the room I first landed in. Behind me, like a magical wind, is Noah right there by my side. He slams the door shut and locks it. Noah looks at me, panting like a dog. "Are you ok?"

I look around the room and nod. "Yes. But, we've got to get outta here."

"No, we can't," he retorts.

"What? What do you mean? Alyssa and those ugly things of hers will find us and kill us."

"No. We must hide, and hide well enough to where they can't find us. Once they tire out and fall asleep, we'll go back. Now, we know where she keeps the rainbow crystal. And we mustn't leave without it. That's why we came here in the first place." His hands rest on my shoulders. "Trust me. It won't be long before those lazy scoundrels get tired."

My body eases up with those reassuring words. Looking into Noah's eyes, for the first time, I really do trust him with my life. "Ok," I say. "Where do we hide?"

CHAPTER SIXTEEN

Getting Back the Rainbow Crystal

WHEN I WAKE UP, I find myself in a dark, dusty room. I peer around me to see where I am—in some sort of basement or wine cellar. There are wine racks filled with wine bottles or bottles with blood, whichever, I can't tell. I must have dozed off for a couple of hours. It dawns on me that while we we're looking for a hiding place, we found a hidden door in the floor of that room —the one when we first entered the castle. Noah and I figured it would be the perfect place. We heard small footsteps roaming around, coming from the top floor at one point. Those ugly creatures were looking for us, but the footsteps stopped a while ago.

Sitting on the floor next to me with his legs propped up, Noah is leaning in on his knees, watching me wake up. "I thought I'd let you get a little shut eye to regain some of your strength. I think the trolls finally fell asleep and gave up looking. I haven't heard noise in a while." He grabs his satchel from around his waist and pulls out the pixie dust. "It's time to give you more of this." he grabs a pinch. "We have some work to do. You ready?"

"I guess so," I rub my eyes and yawn. "I think I'm in need of an energy boost." I snicker.

"Close your eyes." He sprinkles it over my head.

With my eyes shut, I feel the pixie dust tickle my nose; it makes me sneeze. *Achoo!* Once more that familiar tingling sensation takes over and a euphoric rush penetrates through my body. After a few seconds, I open my eyes. "Amazing." I glance over at Noah with a smile. "I'm ready."

I jump up off the ground and fix my T-shirt that is crumpled. "Ok, let's go."

Noah follows me. "Seraphina," he says, but is interrupted by an apparition of some sort, glittering there in front of us, stopping us in our tracks. *It's mesmerizing.*

The beautiful, glittery face smiles at me. She's quiet at first, reaching out her hand as if to touch me. Her glowing, blonde hair is long and wavy and blows from the breeze that her presence creates around her. Blue eyes sparkle and coordinate with a white, flowing gown and a gleaming rainbow aura.

"Josie Lee?" I can feel my eyes grow to the size of saucers, recognizing that face, which I would know anywhere. She seems somewhat different—more peaceful, happier—looking just like an angel. "Is that you?"

"Yes," Josie Lee responds. "I'm here, *always* watching over you. I've never left your side." Her hand reaches out toward me. I reach out to touch it, but can't. It's transparent; it's not a human body. She's a spirit, a sort of ghost, but not. It's weird.

"Alyssa must be stopped," Josie Lee continues. "You have to go now and hurry to bring the crystal back to its home, otherwise Raiven and planet Earth will be destroyed forever. She's pure evil. Go now. They all are still asleep, but not for long."

Nodding, I'm still in shock; not able to move or speak.

Josie Lee gives me one more smile and says, "Don't waste another minute. Go. I am proud of you, Seraphina. I love you." And with those last three words spoken, Josie Lee vanishes into thin air.

"I... I...love you too." I respond, but Josie Lee is already gone. I'm left staring at the empty space where she was just standing.

Noah waves his hand in front of my face. "Did you hear her, Seraphina? Not another minute. Now, we must go."

"She's proud of me?" I can't help but grin from ear to ear.

"Well, of course she is. Why wouldn't she be? Just look at you. You're more courageous than you give yourself credit for."

And for the first time since all of this, I don't feel that afraid anymore. All fears stripped away, like layers on an onion. *Yup. I finally feel courageous for once. There isn't anything stopping me now. Not going to fail you, Josie Lee. Never.*

AS I OPEN the door to where the witch is keeping the rainbow crystal, it creaks. All of those familiar, tiny hairs stand up on my arms. It smells like a dead animal (that's because there is one, still with blood all over it on the table), and there are flies swarming around it, the dead bat, from earlier. But on the opposite side of the room, there sits the crystal—gleaming in its glory —unbothered and simply exquisite.

I'm drawn in by its presence and walk over to it, observing it glimmer all of its colors of the rainbow.

Noah is beside me, staring at it as well. "It's marvelous, isn't it? It's what keeps our world magical and powerful. Its energies are nothing but healing and positive. It's what keeps all the realms connected and balanced. It doesn't belong here. Let's bring it home. Go ahead." He gestures his arm out to the crystal for me to pick it up; I do. I stare and examine its every beam of light—from red, orange, and yellow to green, blue, and violet.

"Why doesn't it do to me what it did to Alyssa?" I examine my hands, unaffected, while holding it. "They're still the same."

Noah chuckles. "Well, my dear, that's because it doesn't need to change you. You're pure at heart, and already young and beautiful."

"Oh, right. Thanks." I reply. *Duh.*

"Well, well, well, look at what the black cat dragged in," a voice says coming from the doorway. Standing there by the entrance is Witch Alyssa and her two, ugly, drooling trolls. "You really thought that you and your gross, smelling fairy friend would just waltz right in here and leave with my crystal?" Pacing the doorway, she puts her hands on her hips. Her once crystal, clear, eyes are now blood-shot red and are squinting evil.

Frozen, my eyes roam from the witch and then over to Noah. I wait to see if he gives me a cue for the next move, but none comes.

Alyssa waves her index finger in the air from side to side. "Uh-uh. Not in my castle, you don't."

I don't know what to say or do next, and Noah isn't saying anything either. "Um, we were just looking at it. Here, you can have it back." I hold it out to Witch Alyssa, shaking like a leaf.

"Oh, my naïve little girl, I know I can have it back, and not only will I be keeping the crystal, but you and that unicorn of yours will stay here with me as well. You fell right into my trap. I didn't even have to venture out of my own backyard to get you, because you came right to me. Just like a moth in a spider web." She thrusts her head back laughing with her arms now held up high.

"As far as that smelly fairy boy, he's got to go!" She points in our direction. Her voice escalates. "Boys, seize them!"

Both trolls charge after Noah and me, and just as they do,

we hear a loud banging on the door downstairs. It's Stella. I can feel her anxiety trying to break into the castle after me.

It distracts the witch and trolls just enough that they jolt around, and Noah has time to reach over his shoulder and grab his bow and arrows. He aims at one troll and shoots. It hits the black, frizzy-haired one right in the middle of the forehead. The troll falls backward to the floor and lands flat on his back. *Smack.*

Noah takes another shot at the other troll—hits him in the heart. The white, frizzy-haired troll grabs the arrow, yanking on it to remove it from drawing out his life, but it's too late. He falls onto his knees and then face-first onto the floor. *Spat.* Blood dribbles out from one side of his mouth. Both of their lifeless bodies now lie there on the cold, hard floor.

My mouth is dangling open. *Holy Mackerel! Noah is pretty good at that. Didn't know he had it in him.*

Alyssa watches both of her trolls go down and die. She begins to chant that strange, unknown language again. Then, raises her arms up to the sky once again and disappears. The only thing left of the witch is a faint laugh from her in the distance.

Noah is searching the room everywhere for her, but she is nowhere to be found. He comes back over to me, where I'm still standing in shock. I feel like I'm in the middle of some scene in an action or horror movie.

He shakes me. "Seraphina, run. Run to Stella. She'll ride you back to safety. I'll catch up with you. You must save yourself and the crystal!" He looks at me, bringing it closer to me and clutching it to my chest.

"But, but, you—" My heart beats a mile a minute.

"Go now!" He demands again.

With the crystal held tight, I run to break free for the outside.

I dart down the stairs, out the corridor, then bust through the front door. Waiting for me is the pleasant, white, angelic sight of my unicorn. I jump on Stella's back, and we ride together like the wind—through night,fog, rain, and mud. I cling to that rainbow crystal for dear life, holding onto it with every ounce of energy and strength I have left.

~

"THE PIXIE DUST. We don't have the pixie dust. How are we going find the door?" I'm looking at my compass; it reads 182 degrees south. It's the right location, but I can't see any door. "Oh no, Stella, Noah still has it. We're doomed." I put my face in my hands, weeping.

This makes Stella upset, and she starts bobbing her head up and down at a rapid speed. "Sorry, girl." Sitting on the ground next to Stella, she then leans down and nudges her cold, wet nose next to my head. I pat the back of her mane."I didn't mean to upset you. I know crying about it isn't going to accomplish anything anyway. We're just going to have to figure something else out."

She licks away my tears.

~

AFTER MY LAST attempt of roaming around with a branch until I hit something hard in mid-air didn't work either, I give up. "It's an invisible door, stupid. You can't feel it." I talk out loud to myself while I doodle in the murky mud with the same wooden stick. In the other hand, I still clutch the crystal, which seems to be losing its glow. I look down at myself all muddy, dirty, and wet, looking like a hopeless case.

Stella is right beside me, nudging my hand with the stick with her nose, trying to offer me comfort. I can feel her.

Not too far off in the distance are a couple of vultures flying low and hovering, hoping that we'll wither up and die at any minute.

"Sorry, girl. I guess I failed us." I brush Stella's face with my hand. "I don't know what else to do. I wish Noah was here."

A soft breeze begins swirling around us, and I smell the strong aroma of gardenias. "Noah?" Glitter glistens in the air in front of us until that small, familiar fairy boy forms back into himself. Standing there with his hands on his hips, Noah crosses one foot in front of the other.

"Noah?" I jump up at lightning speed, tossing my arms around him, even if it is around the top of his head. I knock him over. I've never been this excited to ever see anybody before.

"It's ok, my dear Seraphina. It's ok. I told you I'd be right behind you. I vowed to be by your side the whole time, and I never break a promise." He pats the side of my leg. "Your wish is my command."

"But, how? How did you make it out and get here?" I ask.

"Have you forgotten? I'm a fairy. I fly." He flutters his sparkly wings with a warm smile, bowing. "And a warrior one, might I add. I do my job well."

"Oh, Noah, I did forget how magical you are. I'm sorry I underestimated you."

"Oh, please. You're only human." He gives a subtle wave of his little hand and winks at me.

"Did...did you kill her?" I gnaw at my cuticles.

"No. I searched and searched her castle, but she never reappeared. She is very powerful as well, and knows how to perform magic. But I say this not to scare you," Noah adds, "but to inform you. Alyssa will continue to search for us, and she won't stop until she gets back the crystal. There's a whole army of trolls that are at her beck and call—those two were not the last of them. She will be watching us, so we never know when they will attack. We must act fast and smart. Are you still with me?" His eyelashes bat.

"Of course, Noah. I won't let you down." I mean it with every ounce of my heart, leaping up and down.

"Good." He smirks. "Then, I guess I can give you this now." He pulls the pixie dust out from his satchel. "I believe you were looking for it?"

I nod my head and *sniffle* while wiping away a couple of old, dried-up tears from my cheeks. "Yes, I was."

"What do you say? Want to give it a try?" He holds out the satchel for me to take a pinch of the pixie dust. I stick my hands in it and grab a small amount, heaving the dust in the air. After a funnel of dust forms, the door is now visible, right before my eyes. It was right there all along.

"See?" Noah says. "You got yourself all upset over nothing." He points to it like it was so obvious.

This makes me chuckle. Noah has a way about him that makes everything feel lighter—maybe it's a fairy-thing.

"It's nice to see you smile. You are much prettier when you're smiling."

"Thank you." I'm a little embarrassed, so I change the subject by glancing back at the door, which seems to be waiting for us to make our next move.

"Remember," Noah continues. "It's always good to keep a sense of humor, even in the midst of turmoil. It's a good trait when you can laugh at yourself."

I take a deep breath. "Should we go in?"

"You read my mind," he responds.

"What lies ahead?" I ask him, biting at a loose piece of cuticle.

"I guess you're about to find out." Noah responds. "But first," he sprinkles me with pixie dust, "this."

I feel it tickle the top of my head. I close my eyes and inhale. I re-open them and look down at myself to take notice of dry and cleaned-up cloths. I sparkle and glow, feeling like I just got out of a refreshing shower and made myself all up. "That just amazes me everytime." I beam with delight.

Noah, smiling, gestures with his hand held out toward the door.

"Ok. Well, let the journey continue then." Opening the floating door, I put one leg in, then the other.

"Doesn't it always?" Noah hurdles himself through.

Following right behind us is Stella.

However, this time instead of going down a slide, we shoot upwards—spiraling—at a rapid speed. A strong force of some sort is suctioning us up – almost like a vacuum effect. It feels awesome, like I'm shooting to the sky through some sort of vortex. *So cool. Woo-weee!*

CHAPTER SEVENTEEN

Orange Realm (Land of Gigantic Honey Bees) and Yellow Realm (Land of Sunshine and Sunflowers)

BEES, bees, and more, well, the biggest bees that I've ever seen are swarming everywhere. But, it's not even the bees that I'm that drawn to. Yeah, they're exciting, but it's the gorgeous flowers I can't take my eyes off of. The colors and arrangements are so plentiful and perfect—it looks like a postcard. There are sunflowers, pink daisies and peonies, yellow daffodils, and even different-colored carnations, tulips, and roses—the list seems to go on and on. The flowers soak in the rich vitamins of the sun's potent rays, yet it's not hot or humid, like Florida. As a matter of fact, quite the opposite; there's a cool breeze, yet it's not cold at all. This perfect breeze makes the flowers sway ever-so-slightly, while the bees seemingly dance with them in the process. The bees are in total synch with their pollination process; all of nature together in complete peace and harmony.

Taking a deep breath, I close my eyes for a moment, feeling nature inside my veins. This is a moment I want to take in.

When I open them back up, I notice Noah capturing the sight as well. "I guess this would be the land of the honey bees?" I ask. And as soon as I do, I observe a huge one from a short distance fly right past us. I grip Noah's arm. "Or gigantic honey bees, I mean. Goodness gracious!"

Noah chuckles. "Yup. Not all are that big as you can see, but just mainly the queen bees, whom you do not want to mess with by the way. We have to be very cautious of those big ladies. If they feel any threat to their hives, it could get ugly. And there mustn't be one too far off because they never leave their hives unless they go on to make a new one somewhere else."

I squeeze Noah even tighter, "What do you mean?" I watch the fuzzy, yellow and black jacketed insect investigating a sunflower, and then it flies off. This particular one looks more like a flying, black and yellow tarantula than a bee.

Noah releases my grasp and then rubs my shoulder. "Don't fret. We will not be bothering any of their hives, so we need not worry. They are usually pretty docile most of the time—it's just if they feel threatened." Noah begins walking as if he knows where he's going, and I follow behind him like a lost puppy.

Noah continues. "They really want nothing to do with us. They're more focused on their important job at hand. That's how it is here in our world, Seraphina. We do not want any wars —just peace, unless our species is threatened, which is the case with Witch Alyssa and her trolls."

The second time I gaze at that gigantic queen bee I see it a little differently; it doesn't seem as scary to me. My tension eases up a bit as I follow Noah through this beautiful field of flowers. I caress Stella as we walk side by side. "Tell me more about the bees. They seem so interesting."

Noah almost stops in his tracks. "Interesting to say the least. Bees are by far one of the most important living creatures in the world. Without them, everything would eventually wither away and die, including us fairies and you humans. And even Stella over here who eats plants, fruits, and grass." She wiggles her head. A small gust of glitter flickers off from her horn.

"It's ok, girl." I pause and rub Stella's soft body. "Go on." I want to hear more from Noah now.

"Well, without this simple act of pollination from our furry little friends, our plants wouldn't give birth to seeds and fruits." Noah continues to walk graciously through the field. "Eventually crops would fail, the animal kingdom would collapse, and then we would go hungry, and eventually we would all collapse. So, you see how everything is connected?"

He is so wise and knowledgeable. Noah is like having that friendly teacher whom you just love at school. Being in his presence is a gift.

"I never really thought about it like that before." I stop to smell a yellow rose. "Mmm. And we wouldn't have these beautiful flowers to smell or look at either."

"That's right," Noah continues. "And you want to know the most amazing part about it all?"

"Yeah." I prance.

"They don't even realize they are so special, that the mediocre job that they do every day is saving the planet. They just do it because it's their purpose instilled in them through birth—to collect the nectar; that's it. They do what God intended them to do without question or hesitation. They don't even know it's for a much higher purpose."

Noah brushes along some sunflowers as he passes them by. A couple bees flurry off unaffected.

"Hmm. Even a little bee has a purpose." I stop and examine one of the honey bees on a daisy this time.

"Everyone and everything has a purpose. And that's why it's important that every single one of us live out what that is, because we never know the bigger meaning behind what that purpose is to fulfill. Imagine what destiny we would change if we didn't, or if the bees didn't. That's why it's crucial to live the way we were meant to—all unique, but all very important."

The sun glistens on Noah's peach-colored skin making him glitter in its glorious light. It's such a pleasant sight. It makes me feel safe on some level.

"It's like the psychic told me."

"Psychic?" Noah asks, seemingly a bit confused, but curious.

"No. Just some psychic that Josie Lee and I went to once. She told me that we had a destiny to fulfill that would one day 'save the world'. We didn't believe her at the time. We thought she was crazy, actually." I laugh. "But, now, I believe her." Still holding the rainbow crystal, I draw it in closer to my side.

He turns around and stares at me with intense eyes. "No, Seraphina, she was not crazy. She led you to this path, which is all arranged in the stars—to get you to make that wish that night with your friend, which led you here to Raiven. It is your destiny and the destiny of your friend who passed to the other side." He stops walking and takes both of my hands in his, squeezing them together. "All these events led you here." He possesses a warm grin on his face.

Looking back at Noah with the same intensity, I say, "Yes. I know. I see that now." I loosen his grip a bit by jiggling my hands out.

"We mustn't forget to keep moving, Seraphina." Noah begins walking more swiftly as if we've been wasting too much time talking and observing. "We can't let Witch Alyssa or her trolls find us, and get what they want. Otherwise, Raiven and planet earth with eventually cease to exist as we know it."

I *gulp*. He informs me of this like he went to the grocery store and picked up bread and juice. *No big deal. Just another typical, ordinary day.*

"They know how to get through the invisible doors, and may even be watching our every move through her crystal ball. I'm sure they're planning an attack when we least expect it. That's why we must be one step ahead of the game at all times. Never let your guard down."

I watch another little bee pollinating a daisy. "Noah?" I call to him.

"Yes?"

"I see now that I'm no different from these bees. I see what I'm meant to do and how important it is."

"Well, good. It's about time." Noah says, flapping his wings as they glisten.

I STARE up a gigantic sycamore tree. The sunshine's rays poke through its hollow branches, so we can get a clear view of the massive honey beehive that made its home inside there. This is the first time I've seen a beehive up-close, let alone one of that size. I don't want to imagine what the queen bee looks like—it's too close for comfort. But, I don't have to imagine. Just as I think it, I see it; attached to that hive, guarding it with her life.

Noah puts his arm out in front of me, kind of like what my mom does in the front seat of the car when she comes to an abrupt stop.

"We just entered upon her nest," he whispers. "Not good. I didn't even see it until now. We must slowly back up, and walk away, but showing no fear at all. It can sense fear from miles away."

Oh great. Like that thought is going make the fear just melt away. *Better to not have even put that in my mind at all.*

I take one large step backward to meet the three small ones

Noah just took. "Ok, now slowly turn around and walk the other way." He is still whispering.

Turning around, I trip on a rock. *Oh crap!* I stumble to the ground with a loud, *thump. Shoot. Where did that come from?*

*Oh, no. I can feel it creeping in. The fear. Shut it out...shut it out.*I clamp my eyes shut and am afraid to turn around to see if the queen bee heard or senses me.

"Get up, Seraphina." Noah quickly helps pick me up from the ground. "She's coming this way."

I whip my head around to the sight of a yellow and black tarantula-like bee flying directly at us. Without even blinking, I leap to my feet, and try to get out of there.

"Quick, get on Stella!" Noah shouts.

The two of us hurdle onto Stella's back in a flash. Within a split second, the bee is approaching our rear. Stella hangs a quick right through the field of flowers. The bee veers to the right as well, almost on Stella's tail. It's making a loud, buzzing noise, which vibrates the moving air. *Buzz...buzz...buzz.* This queen bee sounds mean and mad.

Glancing behind him, Noah keeps hold of my waist. He jumps, now standing on Stella's back, and somehow is doing a balancing act on her. He reaches to take his bow and arrows from around his shoulder. Noah aims, draws, and shoots. The queen bee moves, and the arrow misses her. He repeats this two more times, but misses on each shot, until the queen bee turns around and flies back toward her hive in the sycamore tree.

With my eyes clenched, I just worry about continuing to hold onto Stella and the crystal.

"It worked. She's gone. She's gone." Noah is cheering. He sits back down and turns around, while Stella begins slowing down. "She must have realized we weren't a threat anymore to her hive, and that she was risking her own life. Not worth her time. We're safe now."

I'm sweating. "Phew." I take hold of the hair strands stuck to my face and move them off. "I thought you said that they were usually docile."

"Exactly. I said *usually*, not always. We must have taken her by surprise."

"You think?" I reply sarcastically. "Ok, well, let's not do that again then. Plus, I think I've had enough of this land of the gigantic honey bees. It's pretty and all, but can we go find the invisible door now?"

"I think so." Noah runs his hands through his blonde, frazzled hair. "When it comes to things that fly, I think I'll stick to what I know best—fairies."

Stella wiggles her whole body and bobs her head up and down in agreement. "Neigh...neigh." She *puffs* out a large breath through her nose. Even Stella is ready to move on.

WE FIND the invisible door and enter the same way to the yellow realm (land of sunshine and sunflowers), which is just a sunnier, yellower version of the orange realm. The only difference is that the yellow realm is only fields of sunflowers with basically no trees or bees.

Tired and after walking for miles, we decide it's time to take a rest, eat and drink something. We sit down in a field, picnic style. Noah unwraps some fruit from a cloth that he had picked earlier from the orange realm, including oranges, peaches, and even some apricots. Nuts and berries are also stored in there from Fairyland, which he brought along the journey with us; he hands me a couple. I munch on them like a hungry chipmunk.

Stella grazes, while Noah and I decide to have a picnic in a sunflower field. The fruit is juicy and delicious as I take bite after bite of the ripe fruit. *I'm starved.* Juice drips down my lips, and I indulge in it. The fruit is even tastier than where I come from. There is actually no desire to eat meat while I've been here. Maybe it's the oneness I feel with nature, although I haven't even seen that many animals yet. However, Noah explains to me that that is about to change once we enter the green realm (crystal forest). He tells me that there are many elves and fuzzy, apparently adorable animals there including squirrels, chipmunks, and bunny-rabbits.

Noah *crunches* on some nuts and berries, and then takes a bite out of a peach. He also has a jug of water, which we both take turns drinking out of, pouring some water in the cup of my hands so Stella can have some too.

"Where we are now is more of a resting realm. It's the middle-ground of all the realms," Noah explains. "It balances out all of them—the sun is the focus, nourishing all the life around it. It reminds us to stay centered, to find the peace within ourselves, and within the moment. So, here we are." Noah takes another bite of the peach, which matches his skin, and opens his arms out in front of him as he looks around. "Perfect place for a picnic."

I observe it all, soaking in the rays of vitamin D. I've seen pictures from my parents' trip in Tuscany, Italy, and although I've never been there, it feels like to me how that picture looked —just perfect, sunny, and serene. The sun is energizing and glorifying. I can't help but think to myself that back home everyone is always so busy in a rush—even me at times—to not stop long enough and take in all the beautiful nature that exists all around. It really is such a shame. But, I know that I will never take it for granted ever again. If I make it out alive, that is. And then the peaceful thought is interrupted by the important task I still have to finish—get the rainbow crystal safely back to its home with Wizard Arbit Maximus and his castle. *That, and we're not being attacked by anyone or anything. At least, for now. Goodness Gracious!*

I glance over at the crystal, sitting on the ground next to me, which is also taking in the sun's potent rays. It shines a ray beam of all of its crystal clear colors—red, orange, yellow, blue, violet—back at me. *It's so spectacular!*

CHAPTER EIGHTEEN

Green Realm (Crystal Forest of the Elves)

I FLY through the invisible door and out onto a ground of rich, green moss. It covers miles of land, but with trees of all sorts— sycamores, oaks, and willow trees.

The sound of running water vibrates the air. I stand up to observe a moss-covered waterfall, which leads to a cave beneath. It trickles down with a full rainbow, running straight across making the water look like a sheet of glitter. The waterfall runs into a small, heart-shaped pond, where two trees interlock from opposite ends of the pond. They cross paths over it and connect their branches. The trees are covered with blue and purple hydrangeas. And floating happily beneath the trees' branches is a family of white swans. Behind the pond, there are two streams that lead in opposite directions.

Blue jays whistle as they fly above the waterfall, playing with one another. Two fuzzy-grey squirrels chase and chirp at another one up into a tree; one of them has a nut in his mouth, and the other one is trying to steal it from him.

Between the streams, squirrels, and birds, they seem to be in complete harmony together, singing their own blissful song.

My musing over this scene is interrupted when the sound of a flute filters the air. It startles me. "What was that?" I ask Noah.

"It's the elves. They're notifying their people that they have visitors." Noah pauses and then points to himself, then at me. "We would be the visitors."

"Oh." I reply. "Is that a good or a bad thing?"

"Elves are very spiritual, kind beings. They do not harm anything. Unless, of course, they are protecting themselves."

"Oh, of course." I shake my head. I'm not quite sure what that even means anymore.

A bunch of butterflies flutter around everywhere—aqua blue, Monarch, and bright yellow ones. A blue one—my favorite color—flies and lands on my hand, and stares at me for a moment, like the butterfly knows who I am or something. Then it flies away into the sky, which has some purple tones stretching across, sharing along with it some blue, orange, and even pink shades.

I'm lured in by this place's beauty, and can't help but follow another butterfly (a large Monarch) as it flaps around some flowers, through some bushes, and out onto an open field toward the waterfall. It goes behind the water and disappears. I peer behind the waterfall and try not to lose it but instead stumble upon an emerald, green crystal sticking out of the ground. "Oh goodness! What is this?"

I hear a soft, feminine voice out of nowhere. "It's our realm's magical emerald crystal."

"Huh?" I turn around to see a beautiful, thin woman with straight, light-purple hair and the longest, pointiest ears. Her hair touches her waist where her long, flowing, white skirt begins. Her tummy peeks out, showing off her lean figure. She smells of roses dipped in lavender and holds a purple flute in her hand.

I'm taken by surprise. Although, I'm guessing she's one of the elves. I'm not sure whether to run away, hug the striking creature, or say anything at all. I'm a bit awkward, standing there like an idiot, though, so I do what I do well when I'm nervous—bite at my cuticle. That always takes the anxiety away. *No, stop.* Remember what Josie Lee and Queen Ivy say. "Too pretty to have your fingers in your mouth."

"Are you ok?" the elf asks me. "Aren't you the chosen one?"

Shoot. Where is Noah when you need him? And why can't they just say my name instead of the 'chosen one'? Sounds like some hero in an adventure movie or something.

"Uh-huh. That'd be me." I throw the elf a slight wave.

"And what's it to you?" Noah now enters our space from a tiny ball of sparkling glitter-light, forming into his full self again.

Oh, thank heavens! Ok, great, Noah is here to save the day. What in the world took so long?

"Well, what's it to you?" the elf responds, remaining very still.

There's about a five second stare down.

What's going on here? I wonder.

Noah opens up his arms with a warm smile. "Angelica."

The female elf responds with the same welcoming gesture. "Noah. My dear, old friend."

Witnessing this in a state of shock, I wave my finger from fairy to elf, "Um, you two know each other?"

They embrace. Angelica is about the size of me, so Noah's arms barely make it around her waist.

"Well, of course," Noah answers. "What did you think?" He looks at me like I'm an odd-ball.

"Um, I thought you two were in a stand-off, to be honest.

That's what I thought. This place always surprises me." I shake my head.

Angelica and Noah laugh like I was just born under that mound of a rock next to us there on the ground. Talk about feeling awkward.

"Nah." Noah waves his small hand. "Just haven't seen each other in quite some time. That's all."

Angelica laughs again like Noah is the king comedian of all of Raiven.

Really? Oh, come on.

"No. We've been waiting on you two to cross through our realm and with that crystal there with you." Angelica points to me, clasping the rainbow crystal. "And gladly I can see you all made it." She smiles.

I clutch it as close to my chest as possible.

"You see, Noah and I are on the same side. We ultimately work for the good of our realm, this planet, and its creatures. We want to get the crystal back to the wizard so we can all go back to our peaceful ways." Angelica walks closer to me. I take a step back, not knowing Angelica's next move. With one swipe of her tender hand, she caresses the side of my face. "You are brave to have this job. All of us thank you."

Angelica extends her arm out to the forest, and many elves come out of their trees. *But, from where? I have no clue.* It's like they were camouflaged with the trees. They come over to greet me one by one, hugging and thanking me. But they are not short, like I would have expected elves to be; quite the opposite.

Most of them look the same as Angelica, but different genders with different skin and hair colors. However, all of them have long, flowing hair and clothes, even the males—some older, some younger, but with this pose of eloquence and grace.

"Please, come to my home to join us in celebration," Angelica requests.

"Ok. But for what?" I ask curious.

"Well, you made it this far, for one. And you got the rainbow crystal back from that evil witch, didn't you?" she asks, waiting for a response. From the smirks on all the other elves faces, so are they.

"Yeah, guess I did, didn't I?" I grin and notice Noah who is smiling back at me too.

"Well, let's go then. Follow me." Angelica leads the way as we all follow.

A couple of bunny-rabbits peep their heads up from their holey homes in the ground, squirrels come out from the branches, and birds fly above our heads; all to catch a glimpse of the audience that's gathered at this moment here in the crystal forest.

AFTER WHAT SEEMS like walking a lifetime, we finally come upon a large oak tree, with a door in it. The tree even has two small, wooden windows at both ends of the top of the tree trunk, which are open. Moss covers the trunk, so just the door and windows are visible.

Angelica opens the door for us to come inside, which I assume is her home. It's much bigger inside than I imagined it could be. I can't tell that from just looking at it from the outside. It's nothing fancy, but it seems functional. There's a small kitchen with a wooden, rectangular dining room table with six, matching chairs. There's a floating island with pots and pans hanging over it and a small stove.

A spiral, wooden staircase leads the way to a second story, or loft rather, which hosts a full bed. "It's not the biggest place, but it does its job. Gives me room and board for just one," she says.

"It's adorable." I mean it.

Four of the other elves come in as well, while the rest part ways. Stella stays outside eating some of the grass, being she's too big to come inside. We all sit at the dining room table. Angelica takes out some bread, wine, water, fruit, and cheese. "How do you like having a unicorn?" she asks taking a glimpse of Stella.

I glance outside the door, which remains open, to get a view of Stella in her own world, not bothered, yet beautiful. She's like a silk, white dress hanging on a clothing line, flowing to the peaceful breeze, which enters in through the aperture. "It's... *she's amazing.* What's not to like?"

"Have you witnessed any of her powers yet?" Angelica asks.

"Other than she moves as fast as the wind? Nothing much yet."

"Unicorns are the most magical, genuine, powerful creatures on the planet. And you are the one responsible for her existence. Isn't that incredible?"

I really haven't given it enough thought, with everything else going on—the witch and returning the crystal—but now that I think about it, *yeah, it is pretty incredible.* "How or when can I see these magical powers of hers?"

One of the other elves intervenes in the conversation—a male with white hair. Seems to be in his twenties, but I can't tell. "Oh, you can't force it upon a unicorn, they only show it in their own time or when they feel it's very necessary to use."

"Oh, cool." I fiddle with my fork on the table. I snatch one of the ripe grapes from the plate and pop it in my mouth. "May I?" I ask, pointing to a piece of bread and cheese on a platter.

"Oh, please, by all means, help yourself. That's why I put it there." Angelica pushes the platter closer to me. She pours herself a glass of red wine, one for the two other elves, and one for Noah. Noah makes a slight "no thank you" gesture. Then, she pours a pinch in a glass for me. "Just a taste...to toast for you." However, I just wave my hand nicely and decline. *Maybe a virgin strawberry daiquiri. Those are awesome.* I get them pool-side in Florida with my parents while on our stay-cations. Angelica raises her wine glass. "A toast." Everyone else at the table copies her. "Cheers to Seraphina, the chosen one." Blood rushes to my cheeks. "May you guide her through her travels, keep her safe from the evil that lurks, and help her successfully accomplish her important task. May she get the crystal back to where it belongs. And may she return home safely."

"Cheers," Noah responds, drinking a swig of water. The white-haired elf says, "cheers." Another female elf at the table with dark-brown hair, and almost black-olive eyes says, "cheers," in complete harmony. The last to say cheers are the other two elves—identical twin males—both with light brown hair, yellow-green eyes, and they are very cute. They look like they're in their teens. But not sure how old they really are.

All elves sip their wine.

I observe the brood of elves in front of me, analyzing them; their fine features, slender noses, pointy ears, and long faces.

"I'm sorry, Seraphina. Let me introduce you to my crew," Angelica chimes in. "These are some of my finest warrior-elves, like Noah over here." She grins at Noah.

"Hey, but I'm no elf." Noah waves his finger in the air.

"I know, Noah. No offense. Fairies do fly, whereas elves cannot. And we're a little taller." She giggles and winks at him.

My head switches from side to side witnessing this interaction take place between the two. *Funny.* Their kind is really no different from humans; pretty much all the same.

"This here is Marrek." Angelica points to the white-haired elf. "He's one of our greatest acrobats with supernatural strength. It's pretty hard to get a hold of this talented guy."

He extends his arm out and jerks his body around a lot in his chair. "How do you do?" he asks.

I shake his hand. "Good, thanks."

"Then this is Illora." Angelica points to the dark-haired, dark-eyed elf. "She has some pretty keen senses. She can hear, feel, or sometimes even predict what someone else may be thinking or is about to do."

This makes me nervous. I plant my hands over my head like that may stop Illora from getting inside of it somehow. "Um, can you read my thoughts?"

"No, no, no. Don't worry. Not now, usually the gift is only present when the other's guard is down, when they're most vulnerable, or when one is about to inflict pain on someone else." Illora bows her head.

"Oh, ok, good." I throw my hands down along with my guard.

"And these two over here—" Angelica gestures toward the identical twins, "—are Buckthorn and Burdakin, the twin brothers. One can see the other even when the other is not around, which can be of great service. In other words, they always have each other's backs."

The twins are too busy exchanging thoughts in their own inner-world together. One even swipes a clump of some guava jelly and cheese on a big piece of bread, forming a big ball on the inside of his cheek, as he chews with an open mouth. "Hey, how do ya' do?" he asks without even really looking at me.

I don't know whether he's Buckthorn or Burdakin.

"Well, so nice to meet you all. I'm Seraphina, and well, my greatest talent is, um—" I bite a cuticle and then look at it, "—nothing, really. Just being a typical kid, I guess." I shrug.

Angelica places her hand over mine—the one I just bit—and says, "We all have talents. Some of us are just more aware of them than others. You still have time to discover what that is. And by the way, don't discredit yourself. You did manage to wish on a shooting star, birth a unicorn, and steal the rainbow crystal back. You must have greater talents than you realize. Plus, don't you know? Usually it's just the ordinary ones who become the most extraordinary ones." She beams a smile at me.

"You're right." I return the gesture. *I did do all those things. Yet, I keep managing to forget all of it somehow. Does sound better hearing it out loud by someone else, though. It's nice to be recognized.*

"Yeah," joins in Marrek, wiggling his body like he has ants in his pants. "You'll have lots to tell your friends when you go home and back to school."

The twins laugh at each other's inner-jokes, which no one else is involved in.

Then, the voices of everyone at the table become faint sounds in the background to me. The thought of Josie Lee crosses my mind. *Friends? She was my only friend.* I frown with the thought. *Plus, I don't really think if I did tell anyone at school, they'd believe me. Better not to mention it.*

Noah is quiet, sitting next to me at the table, listening to everyone without interruption. He's so considerate like that— such the perfect little gentleman. He's munching on some bread, and my heart feels warm and tingly watching him. I really am growing to love him, like an older brother, even though he is smaller in size. *How old is he?* Noah takes notice of me observing him, and he flashes me a slight smile.

"Seraphina?" My thoughts are interrupted by the sweet sound of Angelica's voice.

"Oh, yeah, sorry. Got lost in thought there for a minute."

"You may want to eat up and then go rest. You can sleep in my bed tonight upstairs." She points to the cozy-looking bed on the loft, which is actually beginning to call my name. For the first time since I've been in Raiven, I can't recall ever feeling this tired, especially after that long walk.

"Yeah, yeah. Try and get some good shut-eye tonight. You'll

need it. No telling when Alyssa or her army of trolls will be on their way. And trust me, they're coming." Marrek jerks in his seat. Just by watching him, I can tell he's ready for a good fight. "But, it's ok. That's why you have us here. We're here to protect you." He raises his fists in the air.

For the first time at the table, Noah enters in on the conversation. "Yes, Seraphina, they're right. Eat and please go rest. We will be here."

"Thank you." I respond to everyone, especially Noah. "But, I'm not that hungry. Just very tired. Think I will take you up on that offer now." I stand up at the table to leave. I am exhausted.

Noah gently grabs my arm before I go to walk away. "I am here, Seraphina." He reconfirms. "I will always be here, and so will Josie Lee. Don't forget to talk to her once in a while. She's listening."

"I know, Noah. Thank you." I reply. Those words bring me comfort.

I walk up the stairs to the loft, and then fall down onto the bed. Peering out the window, I start thinking about and missing Josie Lee. The sun is setting and the sky is now a blend of dark orange, pink, and purple. *It's so beautiful here and peaceful.* I think about what Noah said; about talking to her, and her listening. "Wherever you are, I miss you. I love you."

I lie down on the bed with my arms over my chest, gazing up at the ceiling, which is basically just a brown, tree trunk. My eyes become heavier and heavier; they can't help but completely close. "I love you too," whispers in my ear.

I'm too tired to open my eyes back up; my head turns to the side. "Josie Lee?" I feel myself falling into a deep, deep sleep.

A NIGHTMARE of crocodiles chasing me down and trying to

eat me wakes me up. It's quiet and dark and no one's around. I'm still in Angelica's bed. I look out the window, and there's that grand moon again—the one I saw that night under the willow tree. I stare at it in amazement.

"Seraphina, Seraphina," a familiar voice calls. And there, down below that moon, I see a young, familiar girl with blonde hair.

"Josie Lee?" It looks and sounds like Josie Lee, but I can't say for sure.

The girl waves for me to come and meet her there in the forest under that magnificent moon.

I hurdle out of the bed and dart out the wooden door to her. I embrace her. "Josie Lee. Where have you been?"

"Shhh," Josie Lee responds. "I'm here now." She runs her hands down the sides of my head and squeezes my face together. "Let me look at you."

She gazes into my eyes. But, there's a twinkle in them—one I don't recognize. And I don't recall Josie Lee's eyes being crystal, clear-blue, almost white in color. "Where's the rainbow crystal?"

"It's upstairs. Why?" I try to take Josie Lee's hands off of my face, but her clamp is strong, and her glare wicked. "Ouch. Josie Lee, let me go. You're hurting me."

"Now, now, now, I'm sorry. Didn't mean to hurt you. Just got excited to see you, that's all." She squeezes me again.

Feeling funny in my gut, I loosen up a bit. I'm still not sure what's going on. This doesn't feel like Josie Lee's spirit, but it looks just like her, so it must be her. After all, Noah and Queen Ivy said that I would be able to see Josie Lee at different times, and she did seem somewhat different to me the last couple of times she appeared. This must be one of those moments.

"Can you go get me the rainbow crystal, Seraphina, please? I need to make sure it's safe. It's very important."

The voice even sounds like Josie Lee. "Ok, Josie Lee. I'll go get it. Whatever makes you happy."

Josie Lee sneers at me. "That's right. Whatever makes me happy."

There's that weird twinkle again in her eyes. But I do what Josie Lee asks, because I want to reassure my best friend that the rainbow crystal is safe. Plus, I want to make her proud; that's all I've wanted all along.

Walking back inside Angelica's tree house, I slither back up those wooden stairs and grab the crystal that's in the bed right next to where I was sleeping. I pick it up and examine its glowing beauty,, but I keep getting that gut-wrenching twinge in my belly. I ignore it, walking back down the stairs, out through the door to Josie Lee.

Josie Lee is still gleaming with delight—her eyes bigger than saucers, twinkling at it. It's just nice to see my best friend and see her so happy. She opens her arms and wrenches it out from my hands, roaring out loud with a wretched laugh. It rumbles and shakes the ground from beneath us.

"Yes, yes, yes. It's mine. All mine."

"Josie Lee? What are you doing? What are you talking about?" I tremble.

Before me, under her cloak, the evil Witch Alyssa appears from what once was just an illusion of Josie Lee. The twinkle in her eye intensifies, and an wicked sneer is upon her face.

I GASP FOR AIR, my hand over my mouth, muffling, "Oh, no. What did I do?"

She continues to laugh. "Good girl. You did what you were told. You gave me back what is mine."

"No. No. It's not yours. It doesn't belong with you. It's the wizard's. Give it back to me!" I attempt to steal it from the witch's possession. The crystal sparkles all its splendid colors.

Another set of ugly trolls come out from behind some bushes. It's now obvious to me that they were there waiting for me to screw up and hand it back over to the witch. *How could I disappoint everyone and be so careless?* The signs were there all along. I wanted it to be Josie Lee so badly.

They walk toward me with a big net and two, large swords. They take long, slow strides. They are going to try and capture me. *What should I do?* "Noah! Stella!" *Where are they?* I sweat and tremor. Screaming for them, I use my vocal cords with everything that I have. But, nothing.

The two ugly creatures toss the net over my head and pin me down to the floor. One of them pries open my mouth with his dirty, disgusting, pudgy fingers, while the other holds a vial of some sort of liquid in his hands. The one with the vial pours some of the tangy-tasting liquid in my mouth. "Ekkk. Stop it. Please." I thrash my head around, pleading, and swishing the nasty liquid around in my mouth. Trying hard not to swallow, the one troll clamps down on my lips, pressing them shut. I flail my arms and my legs around, but to no avail; I'm not going anywhere. They have a tight hold on me, and I can't help but swallow the terrible-tasting stuff.

"Stop squirming, you annoying brat." Alyssa is holding down my ankles.

Tears stream down my face. There's nothing I can do; I'm not even strong enough to fight them off. I've failed everyone, including myself. It's completely hopeless.

She just laughs and laughs; the trolls copy her.

"Now, you will sleep...sleep forever." Alyssa holds her arms up to the sky where two strikes of lightning meet each of them, illuminating the blackness. She stands up, grabs the crystal, and glowers at me with that wicked twinkle in her eye again.

"No...no...no!" I kick and scream until I can't any longer. The liquid is beginning to take effect. I can't breathe. No air is getting in any longer, and I hold onto my throat. "H-help me." but the words barely make it out of my mouth. Choking, I start to fade out.

"Seraphina! Seraphina! Wake up!" Noah is shaking my body. My eyelids release open to view Noah with the elves standing behind him, peering down at me on Angelica's bed. However, I still can't breathe, and my arms are flailing at him, not sure who or what I'm fighting off at this point. "Quick!" Noah shouts. "Take her downstairs, outside. She can't breathe."

Marrek picks me up off the bed and bounces with me in his arms down the stairs. So fast, he moves at lightning speed. He situates me down on the cool moss-grass.

Stella plunges her two, front hooves up into the air, quivering her head up and down and side to side. They all must have heard me screaming in my sleep, but Stella couldn't get through into the house.

Illora leans down next to me and touches my arm, closing her eyes. "Yes, I see." She regards the group around us. "Alyssa and her trolls...they got to her through her dream." She looks directly at Noah. "They poisoned her, Noah. She could die if we don't help her."

Noah kneels down next to me on the ground and caresses my hair. "No, no, there must be something we can do. I can't let this happen. I promised her that I would protect her." He rests his elbow on his knee, knuckle to forehead, with his eyes held shut tight. "They knew it. They knew they couldn't get to her because we would be here to guard her, so they used astral travel. Those sneaky scoundrels."

My hands still clasped around my throat, I'm trying with

everything that I can to get any amount of air through my passageway. However, all that I can accomplish is making some loud, *gargling* sounds.

"The unicorn...use the unicorn." An apparition forms, glittering in the sun that's rising over the horizon. I'm fading, and I can't see where it's coming from, but I recognize that it's Josie Lee's voice. I know it's her this time for real, and I can sense her spirit. Her strong force illuminates the air around us, almost like a shooting star, hitting the earth's surface .

Stella kneels before me, next to Noah. She tips her head and points her horn toward my weak body.

"That's it. We will use the magical dust inside Stella's horn. It can reverse the effect of the poison." Noah whirls around to nab his satchel from around his torso. He pulls a pocket knife out of it and holds it to Stella's horn. "Ok, girl, bear with me. This may hurt a bit."

Noah shaves Stella's horn with his knife. She doesn't move, although her breathing is heavy and stressed. Rainbow dust, which resembles glitter, flows out from her horn, onto my face.

I draw in one deep breath, the last one that exists in my entire body, and consume the magical dust through my nostrils and the last open slit left in my mouth. And just like that, my airway miraculously starts to open back up. I gasp for air, sit up, and cough repeatedly. *Kuh...kuh...kuh.*

Illora places her hands over her heart. "It's working."

Noah jumps to his feet. "She's coughing. That's a good sign. It means her airways are opening back up."

Marrek does a back-flip, and the twin boys are skipping and clapping their hands.

After a few minutes of coughing, I take a long look at all the elves. "I can breathe. I'm ok." I turn to Stella who is still in the same position and kiss her head. "Thank you, girl. You saved my life."

Stella nods, but with little movement. She's not her bouncy, bubbly self.

"What's the matter with her?" I ask, shaking her.

"She's just a little drained that's all. Taking away her magical dust depletes a unicorn's energy and powers. Just give her some time." Angelica explains.

I pet Stella with my head held low, and I sob. "I'm sorry, girl. It's all my fault."

"No, Seraphina. Don't do that to yourself. It is not your fault. You were tricked." Noah extends his arm out to me. "Here, now, come. Stand up. Stella will be fine. I promise." He props me up.

I stand to face Noah. "I thought you left me. I called for you...for Stella...and neither of you came. I was so scared." I cry harder.

"I know. I know, poor child." Noah holds my hands. "But, it was just a dream—a nightmare actually. And I heard your cries in your sleep, and I did come to your aid, to your side. And you're here. I'm here now. And look, so is Stella." He points to her.. We're all here now. She saved your life. Josie Lee was guiding us all as well. Just like I've been telling you."

I wipe the tears and snot from my face, "I know. I heard and felt her. She is here. I'm so grateful to you, to Stella, and all of you." I address the crowd that hovers around me, "You have...all of you...really have saved my life." *And I feel more alive now than ever before.*

CHAPTER NINETEEN

The Bloody Battle

A COLD RAG is placed over my forehead. I rest back on Angelica's bed. Noah sits next to my side. "You feeling better?"

"Yes, I am. Thank you."

I love looking at his angelic face and smelling him. *Mmm, that amazing smell of gardenias.* It always makes me feel so warm and safe.

"The rainbow crystal? What are we going to do?" I ask.

"Don't worry about that. Just rest for now. I spoke to Angelica and the other elves. Illora told me that she got a glimpse of Alyssa and her trolls. They haven't made it out of the crystal forest—they haven't crossed through the threshold yet. But they are getting closer, so we shouldn't wait too long. We are to make a plan of attack tonight. And we're going to need your strength." He pats my hand that rests on my belly.

"Ok." Turning onto my side, I shift myself to a more comfortable position. The rag slides off my head. Being I had a restless night of sleep, a nap is very much needed at this point.

Noah grabs the rag and gets up to walk back downstairs to allow me to rest. Before he does, he turns to give me a warm smile, and then leaves the room.

My eyes, weighing heavily, close.

~

THE FLAMES CRACKLE and pop high above the fire pit. We form a perfect circle, sitting around it.

"Let's hold hands," Illora insists. Her dark hair drapes around her shoulders, touching her waistline. She shuts her eyes and reaches out her hands.

Marrek is on one side of Illora and Angelica on the other. One of the twins takes Marrek's hand, while the other twin holds his brother's. Noah holds Angelica's hand and mine, where I join with the other available twin. Stella stands behind us on the outside, under a tree, observing. Her colorful tail swings in the night breeze. She seems back to her normal self.

"The visions are more powerful with the connection of us touching. This way I may even get glimpses of what may happen in the future." Illora takes a couple deep inhalations, concentrating.

"It's ok, Illora, take your time." Angelica confirms.

Illora shifts her body, focusing.

Everyone stays silent for a few minutes. Only the sound of deep breathing, flame crackling, and some crickets chirping are heard.

The stars twinkle like big diamonds in the sky above us in the black sheet of night.

I have one eye open and fidget, waiting.

"Yes, I see." Illora says after three, deep breaths.

"What?" I spring out of my sitting position on the ground.

"Oh, sorry. Didn't mean to shout—just a little anxious." I sit back down.

"As I was saying—" Illora continues. "I see where they are headed. Back by the waterfall, they are making plans to leave through the invisible door shortly. They must have wasted some time through astral travel. Alyssa had to pull some serious magical spells out of her hat to get her and her trolls to do that. But she's gaining more of a force. They have grown in large numbers. There are many more trolls with her now, ready and armed. They will be prepared to fight in case we retaliate."

Angelica appears to be listening to Illora's vision. But it's not long before she intercedes. "Well, we have a strong force here as well with very magical powers. We can take them on." Her job as leader of this pack is to come up with the solution, and I can tell by the eagerness in her tone, Angelica won't stop until she does.

She twirls toward Noah. "Noah, this is where we will need your fairy skills. We can't get there quickly enough by foot to reach them in time before they cross through. You will have to fly and stall them somehow, but I haven't figured out how yet. You are a strong warrior, but not strong enough to take them on all on by yourself."

"Of course," Noah replies.

"Me and the twins can ride Stella and keep up with Noah. She's strong enough to carry us three. "We will be there to fight." Marrek hoists his fist in the air.

"Yup. I'll be on board with Marrek," says one of the twins.

"And I as well," shouts the other.

"Ok, Buckthorn and Burdakin, you both ride with Marrek," Angelica interjects.

"Yippee!" shouts Buckthorn. "Sounds like a game of fun to me."

"Whoo-hoo!" says Burdakin. "Brother-riders of the night." He slaps his twin a high-five.

These guys have got to be kidding. Fun? Only risking lives here, but, hey, no biggie.

"Sorry, Seraphina," Angelica says, "our guys over here sometimes get a little excited to fight. Not much scares them," she says with a puny smile.

"Yeah, I can see that," I respond. "Hey, whatever floats your boat, right?" *Shut up. So stupid sometimes.*

"So, the plan is for me, Marrek, Buckthorn and Burdakin, to ride Stella into battle together, fighting while stalling them. Then what? What about Seraphina, you, and Illora?" Noah points to us. "I don't want Seraphina in the crossfire. She can get hurt. Her only job is to carry that crystal back to the wizard. And I've been hired to see her through that job. That's all. I will honor my queen." His voice gets more serious as he talks.

"I know," confirms Angelica, "and I've already thought about that. I have an idea."

"I know what you're thinking," says Illora. Angelica and Illora lock eyes. Both women show grins on their faces.

"And what's that?" I can feel nervous jitters.

"The dragons," they both say aloud in perfect harmony.

"Whoa, whoa, whoa." I leap to my feet again. "Dragons? Nobody said anything about any dragons. This is where I draw the line. I mean, come on, now. A young person can only handle so much." I brush some ash off of my jeans.

Illora stands up and takes hold of both of my shoulders. "Don't be alarmed. They are nice dragons. They won't hurt you."

"Nice dragons?" I tilt my head, hand on hips, quivering.

"She's right." Angelica stands up as well, so now just the three of us are in conversation with one another. "They are called to duty for the sake of elves, but only in time of dire need.

And I would say this is one of those times. Certain dragons here suit certain elves. Illora and I have our own, and you will stay behind and ride with us."

"Holy crap!" Both of my hands cover my face, because all the blood is rushing to my cheeks. "I can't ride on any dragon. I mean, I just got use to the idea that I can even ride a unicorn. This is insane."

"Seraphina, it's the only way we can do this." Angelica removes my hands from my face. "Unless of course, you have any other suggestions? I'm open to them."

I can see Angelica's concern for me through her eyes. Then, the same with Illora; I know they have nothing but good intentions.

"No, I don't have any other ideas." I pause for a moment. "Ok, guess I'll do it. What does it matter at this point, right?"

We take turns hugging. *Holy crap! This is happening.* I couldn't make this stuff up if I tried—it's better than the storybooks. "Ok, so tell me more about this dragon then. If I'm going to be riding one, I want to know what to expect. I mean, it's not going to shoot fire at me, or anything, is it?" I shrug.

"Not exactly...in the way that you think, at least," Illora says with a snicker.

I don't even want to know what that means at the moment.

Noah and the rest of the group get up from sitting. He pats me on the back. "Good for you, Seraphina. Good for you." He looks over at Marrek, Buckthorn, and Burdakin, "Come on, boys, let's suit and gear up. It's time for us to go and ride Stella like the wind. No more time to waste."

He joins back in on our girls' conversation for the last time. "Ladies, we'll be seeing you soon to join forces. Remember, keep Seraphina out of harm's way, ok? And be ready to take down Alyssa and her army of trolls. We'll be there fighting."

~

WE SEEM to have been traveling for quite some time to get to this place. "Where are we going?" I ask Angelica and Illora who are taking me into a deep part of the crystal forest.

Angelica swats a tree branch out of her path. "To the dragon's cave, where they live."

I swallow hard.

"Don't worry, Seraphina. They will not harm us." Illora brushes my arm as we walk.

We approach a rocky mound with a large, dark gap. If I were to stumble upon this cave alone, you couldn't pay me enough money to go inside. *The black unknown is too terrifying.* "I'm not going in there, am I?" I point to the large gap that looks like it may lead to the center of the earth, or even to the middle of nowhere.

"Not yet," Angelica responds. She puts her arm out to stop me. "Illora and I will be entering first. You stay put for a moment." Angelica hands me a lantern—one of the two that she's holding.

What?

Angelica and Illora tiptoe inside and disappear into the blackness with the one lantern they have left. I watch as the light slowly fades into the darkness.

Goodness Gracious! I'm alone for the first time since I've been in Raiven; truly alone. I don't know what to do with myself, so I go to bite a cuticle, but stop myself in the process. *Nah. Don't need to anymore.* I feel like if I've reached the point of getting to ride on a dragon, then cuticle-biting doesn't really go hand-in-hand with that. *Time to grow up.*

The lantern is pretty much the only light in sight, besides the moon and stars. I gaze up at the sky and study its gloriousness. *Is the moon always full here?* Noah and Stella race across my thoughts. *What are they doing at this exact moment?* I picture Stella running wild, wind blowing her colored mane and tail, and Noah as a sparkling ball of light somewhere, flickering around—ready to conquer the world, like the warrior that he is. *He's so amazing. Have they gotten to where Alyssa and her trolls are? Will they be able to handle them?* And at that moment, I can't help but to pray to whatever God out there hears me. "Please, keep them safe."

"Seraphina." My thoughts are interrupted. Angelica comes out from the darkness with a small gleam of light accompanying her. She gestures and waves for me to head toward the cave opening. "Time to come with us."

"Are...are...you...sure?" I really don't want to go inside, so I'm hoping Angelica changes her mind or something. The thought of what I'm about to see is mind-boggling—dragons with teeth the size of Jaws and fire that will singe my hair to my roots.

"Yes, yes, I'm sure. It's ok." She keeps waving me down from the entrance.

Oh shoot!

My knees wobble as I step inside. It's completely dark, just like I imagined it would be, but the lanterns do light our steps. The cave's rocky walls and sandy ground don't seem interesting, but then something changes as we continue deeper inside. Crystals and stones start dazzling on the walls. Then, we come to a huge cavity. The room completely lights up; there's no need for our lanterns anymore. The emerald crystals are all over the ground and gleam like florescent lights. They look just like the one I stumbled upon when I first entered this realm, but they are twice the size of that one. Between some of these crystals, lie humungous eggs. They have pearl-like textures – some blue, some purple, some green. *These must be dragon eggs.* Not that I've ever seen one before, but I assume that's what they would look like.

"Seraphina, over there." Angelica points to the corner of the room, away from the eggs. I whisk my head in the direction where Illora is standing with two, massive dragons, one on each side.

"That there is my dragon, Saphira Icebreath—Champion of the Blue." Her eyes narrow in on the one who is long and lean with black and blue-toned lizard skin. Her wings are enormous, aqua-blue, with hints of purple at the base. They look like gigantic butterfly wings. Her tail is long and wraps around her entire body; black spikes line the whole base of her spine. Her eyes are slanted with long, feathery, blue eyelashes. *She's breathtaking*. Literally. I feel short of breath just by looking at her.

"She's called Icebreath because her powers can take someone's breath completely away, draining it until death. That or she blows ice out of her mouth, instead of fire, which can freeze you solid. It can last for hundreds of years."

"Oh," I budge a step or two backward.

Angelica chuckles. "Only if she chooses. She knows you're my friend. She can sense it."

"Oh, good. And, the other dragon?" I *gulp. This one looks much scarier.*

"And the other one belongs to Illora. His name is Lyth 'Powerful One'—Lord of the Brown." Angelica directs to the other dragon whose wings stand high above his body, hovering like bat wings. Lyth's brown, orange-red skin has a leathery texture—like a dinosaur's body. His hind legs are raptor claws, yet his front ones are more monster-like. He has tiny white spikes sticking out from every angle of his tight body frame, and two tall antlers peak out at the top of his head. Lyth's tail ends with an arrow shape.

"Lyth is called 'Powerful One' because he shoots deadly fire out through his breath. No creature is too big for his claws to pick up from the ground and dispose of wherever he chooses.

He has no patience for evil-doers. He leaves none alive." Angelica begins walking in their direction. "Both of these special dragons know and sense the difference between the good and the evil. So, believe me, they know who and what to aim for."

I follow Angelica, taking tiny steps, until we stop in front of Illora and the two dragons. Both dragons position their noses up to me. I flinch and seal my eyes tight, feeling the breath of Saphira first—a cold rush of breath, of icy smoke, releases in my face. It feels as though a freezer has been opened; releasing the cold, trapped air.

"Just let them smell you. They want a chance to get to know who you are, to feel a connection," Illora says.

I wince to large, flared nostrils. Saphira bats her eyelashes at me and then raises her head back up in the air. I observe Saphira's every move, unsure about what the next one might be. Lyth copies next, smelling around my hair, but this feels much different. It's like I just walked into a steam room. The overwhelming amount of heat makes me sweat in an instant; water drips down my face. *Please don't shoot fire, please don't shoot fire.* Lyth makes a large sound with his breath. *Whoof...whoof...whoof.* Then, he pauses, backs up a couple steps, and allows room to bow his head at me.

"See," Illora says. "They both like you. They scanned and can read your soul. And they know you're here to help and protect their home. So, they work for you now too." Illora pets the side of Lyth's massive body.

I notice Lyth's protruding chest, with his head held high to meet that of Saphira's—both of them now non-threatening to me. I'm no longer afraid. Lyth even looks like a gentleman, or gentle-giant, rather. I can sense their respect for me.

"We mustn't waste time," Angelica says to us, caressing the side of Saphira's scaly body. It reminds me of an alligator's skin

—those creepy animals, which freak me out. Yet, I don't feel any dislike toward Saphira at all. In fact, quite the opposite.

"Seraphina, you'll ride Saphira with me," Angelica says.

I was secretly hoping this was who I'd be riding. Something just feels more comfortable on an ice-breathing dragon rather than a fire-breathing one. *How silly does that sound?*

"Yeah," Illora adds. "Riding Lyth can be tricky, even somewhat dangerous. His heat can become unbearable if you can't withstand it. And if he picks up any of those trolls, he may play with them like a cat with a mouse. But, I can handle it."

"Hey, no worries. It's all you," I say to Illora. "Plus, riding Saphira sounds pretty cool to me anyway. Haha. That's funny." I laugh at myself. Angelica and Illora giggle. "And she's so pretty." I stare at her feather eyelashes, as she bats them at me.

"Ok, so we're ready then?" Angelica asks.

"Yup, I guess so." Gazing up at Saphira, with my hands in the pockets of my skinny jeans, I'm thinking, *How in the world am I going get up there?*

"When we get outside the cave, Saphira will make it easy for you to get on. I can see you're nervous, but don't be. Saphira will take good care of you." Illora says, reading my thoughts.

"So, let's get moving. We can't keep Noah and the others waiting. They can only hold off our enemies without us for so long." Angelica turns to walk back out of the cave.

"Of course," I'm anxious myself to leave. I shuffle some dirt around with my feet. "Can I ask you something first?"

"Sure. What's that?" Angelica looks over her shoulder at me, walking next to the dragon.

"What in the world are those things?" I throw my hand toward the eggs that we passed coming in.

"Those are incubating dragon eggs." Angelica explains. "They are waiting to be born and connect with their elf. It's actually a destined relationship—kind of like a soulmate. But, first the dragon and elf have to mature enough. However, they just know it when they meet. It's an electric connection."

"Uh-huh." I smirk. "Oh. You don't even have to explain it. I totally get it." The thought of Josie Lee crosses my mind.

～

WE *SWOOSH* THROUGH THE TREES, past the clouds, and that brilliantly bright moon—on a dragon—is the most exhilarating feeling in the world. "Whoo-wee!" I shout out to the night sky.

Clinging on to Angelica's waist, I can feel how Angelica and Saphira are completely in synch and compatible. There is no struggle. It's a flight as smooth as silk. My hair blows with the rush, and the cool air soothes my face. I turn my head to the side, and get a glimpse of Saphira's huge, blue-purple wing, flapping forcefully. One swat of that wing alone could kill someone.

To the back side is Illora riding Lyth; it's the same thing. They are in complete oneness with each other. There's no need for talk; I can tell that they can feel what the other needs or senses—it reminds me of my relationship with Stella.

From a short distance away, there on the ground, is an army fighting. But, being we are so high up, it looks like those little soldier toys that children play with. Except, one is a fairy, and three are elves, and the rest are a number of ugly trolls. But, wait. *Where is that wretched Witch Alyssa?*

I suddenly notice a little head of blonde hair wobbling all over the place. Trying to follow it is difficult, because it moves so fast. The blonde bobble-head shoots his bow and arrows left and right; Noah hits and kills troll after troll. "There." I point below. "There they are. There's Noah."

Then, I spot white, flowing hair waving around everywhere. Marrek is doing acrobatics in the air; flipping, tumbling, and even doing some type of martial arts. He is killing trolls with his sword. Two trolls approach him at the same time; one aims its poisonous arrow at Marrek and throws it toward Marrek's head, but he does a backbend in mid-air, which looks like it's taking place in slow motion. It misses Marrek by an inch. The other troll charges after him by jumping high in the air to pierce Marrek's heart, but he does a spinning, karate-like kick then slices the head off of the troll with his sword. The tongue of the troll hangs loosely out of its disgusting mouth as its bloody head rolls down on the floor like a bowling ball.

The twins, back to back, help each other to fight them off. They do not leave each other for a minute—one constantly communicating with the other about every troll's position. The twins swat them off like flies, slicing and stabbing each that approach with their swords. It's not a fair fight for the trolls, except for them out-numbering the elves. The trolls seem to be coming from everywhere, almost like these creatures keep reproducing from some hidden place among the forest. The elves and Noah fight with everything that they have, yet it's only a matter of time before they will grow tired. They will not be able to keep up with this pace for too much longer.

"Quick! They need our help." I holler from the back of Saphira.

"You go." Angelica yells over to Illora who is flying on Lyth next to us. "I'm taking Seraphina to a safe spot below, and then I will come meet you to finish them off."

Saphira shoots down toward the forest below, away from the bloody battle. "Noooo!" I cry out. "Please, I want to help."

"Seraphina, there is no way you can help. You are not physically strong enough to fight them off. They will kill you. It's our job to keep you safe." Angelica lands Saphira between two, oak trees.

She points to some hedges nearby where she commands me

to wait. "You stay put here. And I promise, we will be back to get you. Call for Stella, so you're not alone. She can sense you and will find you, and when she does, both of you wait here for us." Angelica gives a slight kick to the side of Saphira to take back off into flight. "Whatever you do, do not come back over there. We will handle it." They both fly away, gone into the darkness.

I'm shaking with fear—alone, in a forest, in an unknown place. The only light is the moon now. At least last time I had a lantern. I clench my fist to my chest, squeeze my eyes shut, and take a deep breath. "Ok, just breathe." I inhale five, extended breaths. "Focus. She will sense I need her." After a long pause, I take one more breath and telepathically call for Stella. I focus on her, telling her in my mind how much I need her, concentrating. *Stella, Stella, Stella.*

A few minutes pass. Nothing. "It's not working," I whimper.

The wind makes a rustling sound; it rattles the hedges. Giving me the chills, I don't know who's around or what lurks. An owl hoots every so often, and wolves howl at the moon.

My head snaps around as I hear a loud *crackling* sound of some branches from a short distance away. Footsteps are getting closer and closer. I hug my knees into to my chest. Any animal or creature of the night could just come and eat me—flesh and bones. But it doesn't matter anymore anyhow. I have nothing now to lose – no friends, no unicorn, no weapons, no crystal —*nothing. That's it.* Whoever it is can kill me here, and no one would even know. But, I decide to accept my fate; I'm ready to die if I have to. I tried to succeed for my best friend and failed, and it doesn't matter anymore. I don't even know if Noah, Stella, or the elves, will come out of this alive. The thought alone makes me just want to die.

The footsteps grow louder, and louder, and louder. I squint one eye, while keeping the other open, having to see who or what it is that's going to kill me. And then I catch it, a glimpse, of a pretty rainbow-colored and silky-white, glowing body. It's Stella! *Thank heavens!*

I shoot to my feet and throw my arms around her neck. "Oh, girl. You came for me. You came." I repeatedly kiss the side of her face. Stella bobs her head.

"But, how did you find me?" I ask her like she can talk and respond, but I can sense she understands everything. I know that Stella felt her way to me.

"We must go back and help the others." I say to her. "You have to take me to where they are." I gesture for her to get low, so I can get onto her back. Stella kneels down, and I swing one leg over and leap on top of her. "Go, girl, go!" I slap her on her backside to get her moving.

Funny thing. This once, cuticle-biting girl now wants to help in a bloody battle against a treacherous witch, her trolls, dragons, elves, and a warrior fairy. I guess I'd say, I've come a long way. No more cry-baby, scaredy-cat. Josie Lee would be proud.

THE BATTLE SCENE is even bloodier when we arrive. All the elves are still standing, warding, and killing off the trolls, but I don't see the witch anywhere.

Above are Angelica, Saphira, Illora, and Lyth, swooping down from the starry sky to take turns blowing fire or ice to help Noah and the elves below. None of them seem to see me watching, because they are too preoccupied with their fighting.

At one point, Saphira exhales a storm of ice out of her forceful mouth, and with one blow, freezes three trolls solid.

Lyth dives down, scooping up a troll with his powerful raptor claw, flies out to the middle of nowhere, and drops him down a rocky cliff into the distance.

Saphira is back at it again, but this time flies down to the ground. With her two front legs, she swats at a troll and gets him down on his back. He fights and screams. And as he does, Saphira sucks his breath until the life is drained completely from his body. Now, he's still. She takes back off until she swoops up another one, doing the same thing all over again. Angelica is grasping Saphira's back.

Lyth is shooting out fire flames with his breath, blazing trolls on fire, and in the crossroads burning through moss, grass, hedges, and trees. A scorching fire burns through the magical forest, forming a flame circle around the battlefield. Gasping from the sight, I pray for an end, for a resolution. But I feel help-less. *What can I do?*

Someone snatches the back of my hair and throws me down onto the ground. I smack my back. "Ouch." With dread, I peer up to see that familiar villainous twinkle coming from crystal, blue-white eyes.

Long, wavy, red hair bends down and covers my face. "You're mine now." It's the sound of evil. "You and your unicorn are finally mine." Five of the ugliest trolls, drooling out of their mouths with piercing teeth through their bulging, uneven lips, throw a large net over Stella. They tie her feet together. Stella tries to put up a good fight, but the witch holds a blade to my throat. "If you move or try any magic, dumb unicorn, I will slit her throat with one slice." Stella lies perfectly still.

"Nooooo!" I scream.

Alyssa swings me up by my hair, bringing me to my feet. She continues to hold the knife to my throat. "Let's go, boys. We need to do this and do this fast. I have all I need now to make my power complete and please my evil god. Forget everyone else." She lets out that loud, piercing laugh that vibrates the air. "But we have to go deep into the forest where no one will see us."

The trolls have a rope connected to the net where they drag

Stella against the ground. They don't care what stands in their way. Watching this dreadful site, I can't help but cry out. "Please, let her go. She's just an innocent unicorn. She has nothing to do with this. You can have me. You don't need her. Please." I beg and plead with the witch. "Sacrifice me to your god."

"Shut up, stupid child." Alyssa grasps my hair even tighter. My head is now bent over to one side, while the knife is at my throat. The witch is controlling my every move. "Of course, I need the unicorn. I will be sacrificing both of you, and then giving up the unicorn's horn to please my god." Her crystal whitish-blues twinkle pure wickedness.

CHAPTER TWENTY

Into the Blue

THE EMERALD CRYSTALS are spread out around us in an open space in the middle of the forest. The trolls drop the rope and kick the weak body of Stella, leaving her beaten and bruised from the rough ride. I can't bear to see her suffer; I cry, feeling helpless. Again, I failed everyone. Angelica told me to stay. *Why didn't I listen?* All I wanted to do was help Noah and the elves in some way. But, the only thing I did was find myself in the face of trouble again.

"Untie the unicorn, boys." Alyssa demands to her trolls. Opening her arms up wide and tall to the skies, she speaks that unknown language. I can tell by the dumbfounded expression on the trolls' faces that they're just there to do as she says. They don't have any brains; they're her puppets.

The sky flashes with lightning and it thunders. Rain begins pouring down on us. And it's not soft sprinkles, but a hard downpour. The witch is soaking wet; her hair clings to her face, and her black, eye make-up smudges down her cheeks. The whites of her eyes become redder, and her blue eyes whiter. "By the powers of fire and death, I have here for you the unicorn and the chosen girl. Devil take me...take their souls!" Lightning flashes across the night sky.

There is no voice or sound signifying there is any existence of any heinous god, or devil, but she is worshipping something, and whatever it is, isn't good. *Maybe some sort of black magic?* Her chants become louder, faster, and more repetitive. She holds the knife up to the sky and clenches her eyes shut, repeating these foreign words over and over again. The rain is beating down on her face. After a few minutes of this, Alyssa walks closer to the unicorn that is lying on the floor very still.

"No! Please. No!" Two wretched-looking trolls hold me back as I struggle to break free. Alyssa slowly glides over to Stella, making disgusting, slurping noises with their mouths. The witch prepares to pierce Stella in her throat with the knife.

Holding the blade high in the air, she opens her eyes and looks down with an evil glare, shrilling into Stella's fragile soul. Alyssa slithers her arms downward as she is about to penetrate Stella's main artery, which is pulsating back at her. The witch's eyes heat up with the sight. I shriek even louder. "NOOO!"

But then, out of nowhere, an arrow darts faster than a human eye can catch and pierces one of the trolls in the back of the head who's holding me. He falls face first; his forehead strikes the ground. Then, the other troll leaps to his feet and whips around, grabbing his bow and poisonous arrow swiftly that's wrapped around his fat, short frame; ready to charge at whatever it was that killed his ugly companion. Another arrow whizzes right past me and lands between his eyes. He falls back dead as a doornail.

This gives me just enough time and leverage to charge after Witch Alyssa like a bolt of lightning. I pounce onto the witch's back, and we both tumble to the ground. She ends up on top of me with the knife held high up in the air ready to pierce my heart. But, I fight Alyssa's arm back with every ounce of strength I have. Feeling my face turn fire red, I fight to catch my breath. My teeth grind. Spit starts to trickle around my mouth from me straining so hard. A strong force from nowhere tosses the witch high up in the air, and she lands with a loud *thump*, smacking her back to the ground. The force thrusts the knife out of her hand.

I hear that familiar voice again of my best friend, "Hurry. Get her knife, Seraphina."

I leap to my feet and hurtle over to the witch, snatching up the knife. Alyssa jumps to her feet. Her eyes are hungry with anger, and red veins throb under her white skin. We circle each other. "Go on, you stupid, little girl, try and kill me. You can't do it." She snarls.

An arrow from behind strikes through Alyssa's heart, and she grips onto it with both hands. Her eyes bulge from her face, her mouth dangles open, making *gurgling* sounds. A streak of blood dribbles down the side of her dark, red lips. She falls to her knees and curls over on her side, taking a couple more struggling breaths and dies. Her eyes remain open with that same glare of malice in them.

"She won't have to." A three-foot high shadow in the distance says; bow and arrows by his side, heart-warming, yet solemn look upon his face. I drop the knife by my side and fall to my knees.

The bloody sight around me—the dead witch and all the remaining lifeless trolls with arrows through them are finally finished. They must have gotten hit by Noah in the midst of my fight with the witch, and I didn't even notice.

I cup my hands to my face, weeping.

Noah walks over to me and caresses the top of my head. "It's ok, Seraphina. It's ok. It's over. They're all dead. The witch, she's dead. She can't hurt you anymore."

The rain has now come to a complete stop, but we're drenched. I'm face to face with Noah. The wet strands of my hair cling to my cheeks and the back of my neck. I wrap my arms around his little, yet powerful body.

Stella is still, lying on the ground. "Stella!" I race to her side. "She's really hurt, but she's still alive. I can see her breathing. What do we do?" Panting heavily, I'm frantic, looking around for some sort of clue.

At that moment, a glowing light forms there illuminating the dark forest. It glistens in the night like fireflies. "Use the crystal." The light points to the rainbow crystal, lying on the ground, next to the dead, witch's body.

I scramble and pick up the crystal and then hurry back to Stella's side.

"Let it do its work. Touch her body with it." It's Josie Lee.

I touch the rainbow crystal to Stella's motionless, bloodied, and poor, beaten body. It lights up all of its colors of the rainbow —red, orange, yellow, green, blue, and violet. It shines its light and energy on Stella, and I watch as it completely heals her wounds and bruises. It makes all the rainbow colors in her mane and tail light up and sparkle as well. They're both glittering all the colors together. It's like they belong together. It takes a moment, and when the light diminishes, Stella's eyes open and she squirms. She breaks free from the net that binds her with one vast whip of her powerful, now healed body.

I hug my unicorn around the neck, "It's working. Stella... you're alive!" Stella picks her head up, wobbling around a bit, but does manage to get up onto her feet. She nestles her head into my neck, and we spend the next few minutes nuzzling and cuddling each other.

I turn to face Josie Lee who is watching and beaming at me.

"You now have all you need. The witch is dead. You have Stella and the crystal. Take them to the wizard. He is waiting for you." Josie Lee turns to walk away.

"Josie Lee?" I call out.

Josie Lee twirls around effortlessly. "Yes."

"Will I ever see you again?"

"Of course. But my work here is done for now. I am always here...around...watching over you. My spirit holds no time or space. Its boundaries are limitless. Til' we meet again, and go on more wild adventures together." Her face lights up, and she smiles with those brilliant, bright, white teeth and a glistening, angelic glow.

I always want to remember her just like right now, and hold onto this image forever. *She's so beautiful. She's really an angel.*

I let some loose tears fall down my cheeks and then wipe them off. "Josie Lee?" *Sniff. Sniff.* "I love you."

"I love you too. I'm proud of you, Seraphina. You were always more courageous than you realized. Never forget that you're special." She smiles as her hair blows like a supermodel in the air. She winks at me,, then turns to go. Her flowing, white, dazzling gown vanishes with the sight of her into the deep forest.

I'm taken by surprise when I notice everyone there all of a sudden—Angelica, Illora, Marrek, the twins, and both massive dragons. I'm not even sure how long they've been there. Noah takes hold of my hand. "You ready? Let's finally return the crystal back to Wizard Arbit Maximus so we can get you home."

"How did you know where she took us?" I ask him, still sniffling.

"I heard your cries and saw her take you and Stella. Then, I followed and waited in the distance for the right moment to act —to kill them."

"Thank you, Noah. You saved us." I hug him again. This time even tighter.

"I told you," Noah says, "I would never leave your side, that I would always protect you, and I swore by it. Plus, my dear, I saw you fight the witch. You're pretty brave yourself." Flickering his wings and wearing a big grin on his face, he squeezes me tight as well.

Yeah, I am. I beam back.

THE FLOATING, invisible door awaits us. It's time for Noah, Stella, and me to leave the crystal forest of elves and enter into and pass through the blue (water realm). I must get back the rainbow crystal to its owner, Wizard Arbit Maximus, and that's the way to him. *Whoever that is?*

All of my new elf friends wait to say goodbye, one by one. I give them each a kiss and can't help but give a kiss and a pet to each of the dragons as well. Again, Saphira bats her blue eyelashes, and Lyth bows his gigantic head at me. "Goodbye, friends. Stella and I wouldn't be alive right now if it weren't for your courage, bravery, and loyalty. Thank you. I will always remember and cherish all of you. I hope we see one another again." Waving one last goodbye with those words, I enter the open, floating door, leaving behind another realm—another chapter—to embark on a new one.

"Thank you, Seraphina. We will always remember you," says Angelica. All the others nod, acknowledging her words.

Up, up, and away we go through the vortex—the spiral upward slide—to another place and time, or no time rather, being it doesn't really exist in Raiven. I still can't wrap my head around that concept.

I'm starting to become homesick. I'm ready to see my family

again. *What are they doing?* I wonder. However, I know that still isn't possible yet. I have to journey through one more realm to get where I'm going. *What am I about to encounter there?* I'm exhausted just thinking about it.

We fly out of the invisible door and land on some sort of... old, wooden, broken-down deck? I take a long, good look around me. "A pirate ship?" I ask. A large, steering wheel, sails, mast, and bowsprit...*yup, it's a pirate ship alright. Oh boy.* It's not like I have ever been on one before, but I have read about them and seen all the *Pirates of the Caribbean* movies and know what one looks like. Now, I just wait for a one-eyed pirate with an eye patch to wobble out from some hidden doorway that we haven't noticed yet. But there is no one; it's completely abandoned.

"Seems like we're all alone here in the middle of the ocean. Take a look." Noah is pointing and observing overboard. I stand up and inspect the aqua-blue vastness that Noah is referring to. Stella is trying to keep her balance from the motion of the swells passing beneath us.

"Good grief! Where are we?" I clamp on to the side of the ship, trying to keep my balance as well.

"Well, definitely the water realm."

I shoot Noah a look with a closed-mouth grin and tilt my head a bit. "I get that," I say. My arms open up to the ocean out in front of us. "But where in the water realm, exactly?"

"I'm not sure. I've never been here before; never had the need to, so I'm just as lost as you. It's like you living in the United States doesn't mean you've been everywhere." Noah rubs his chin.

Hmm. Good point. He knows the United States? Of course he does, little know-it-all.

"Great. Is that your only plan? Lost as me...to sail alone at sea? Til' when... til' where? How do we find the invisible door?"

Some motion sickness is setting in; I'm feeling queasy. Either that or the recent events that took place are still lingering in my head. Placing my hand over my mouth, I hold back the urge to puke.

"Calm down. I have the map and the compass. We'll find it. Just make sure you don't lose the rainbow crystal. Let's put it somewhere safe. And please don't get sick."

I release my hand from my mouth for a moment. "Um, that's what I'm trying not to do. Can't you tell?"

The crystal is on the floor by my feet; I pick it up. We search around the ship until we find an old chest. It *creaks* open. Nothing is inside but some salt water, two scattering crabs, and a little bit of old dust.

"Ok, good," Noah says. He pulls out the compass and map from his satchel.

It's daylight now and the sun is glaring down its potent rays. At least the air is cool and crisp, like it always seems to be in Raiven with a few exceptions. However, it is a little hotter than most of the realms—maybe because the sun is reflecting off of the water. I sit on the main deck, under the shade of the main sail, waiting for Noah to come up with a plan.

I listen to the sound of the waves hitting the bottom of the boat, and seagulls sing their chorus through the ocean air. Noah is examining the map and mumbling something in a low voice to himself. His small hand continues to rub his chin as he looks down at the map, taking occasional breaks to peek back at the open ocean. It's as if the answers will just pop out of the water and into his head.

I blow my bangs out of my face.

Stella has surrendered to the ocean's motion and laid down to rest.

Out of nowhere, I'm startled by a huge splash that sends a surge of water into the ship. Again and again, I hear and see all this water making its way into the boat. I leap up and glance overboard to catch a glimpse of some sort of iridescent, blue-green...*mermaid* tail? A female, human body makes its way out of the water, going back down, smacking her tail on the water's surface behind her. The water hikes its way up, thrashing me in the face. I wipe the water out of my eyes to see a beautiful, young woman with the lightest, blue-green hair and eyes staring back at me. A pearl headband holds her hair back in place, and she sports the brightest, whitest smile to match. She waves just like Miss USA. *For the love of...*

Noah pretty much has the same expression on his face that I feel inside; surprised, taken aback. "Did you know that there are mermaids here?" I ask him.

"Ahem," Noah coughs a bit. "Yes, I did, but just never saw one before. She's quite lovely." He has a grin on his face that stretches from ear to ear, and his ears begin to perk up. He's even blushing. His wings behind his back sputter and shed glistening glitter in the sunlight, which traces them.

I scan my eyes from Noah's bewildered face back over to the mermaid who is still waving at us from a short distance. The mermaid does a leap, dives back into the water, and swiftly swims over to us, getting closer. I lean over the side of the ship to get a better look of the mermaid underwater, but can't. The mermaid bursts up through the surface with water beads, saturating her face and hair. She opens her eyes and bats off the last couple of droplets of water from her long eyelashes. Her lips are rosy pink. Crisscrossed around her upper arm, is a pearl bracelet. "Hi." Even her greeting sounds refreshing, like it just got an exhilarating rush through a replenishing, good swim.

Noah and I are now both leaning over the ship, holding on to its side. "Umm, hi," I say. *Real slick, Seraphina.*

"Well, hello, there," answers Noah.

"My name is Bella...Princess Bella. I am ruler of the water

realm here." The mermaid's breathing is a little fast. The water drops trickle down her face one by one.

Princess Bella just may have the most beautiful face I've ever seen. She has a skin tone as white as snow, button nose, thin face and chin, and slanted, blue-green eyes. Her cheeks have a natural pink hue to them to match her lips. Bella is the perfect name for her.

"I'm Seraphina, and this is Noah." I gesture to Noah who is speechless. The perfect gentleman iscaught off-guard and at a loss for words for once.

"Yes, I know who you are." Princess Bella smirks. "I've heard all about you, and what you've done. I know you're passing through with the rainbow crystal, and I'm here to help show you the way. It could be quite tricky with all this water, and everything looking the same." She cackles, and her tail splashes around behind her.

"Oh, that would be awesome. We could definitely use the help. Thanks so much." I swat Noah in the shoulder to sort of wake him from his dazed state.

He shakes his head. "Oh, right, yes, that would be great." Noah finds his composure and clears his throat again. "Ahem. Yes, my compass and map here tell me that the invisible door to get to the violet realm would be about two-hundred eighty degrees northwest?" *There he is. Mr. Professor.*

Princess Bella chuckles again. "Oh, I'm not sure about all that now. I would know based on my memory and instinct. I've been traveling through these waters for many, many decades."

"Oh, of course, Princess." Noah nervously tries putting his map and compass back in his satchel. "You just lead the way then, and we'll follow."

"Sounds like a plan." Princess Bella smiles at us, swimming backward, using her powerful tail. "One of you just needs to steer the ship. Who's going to be captain?" Water splashes and spirals all around her, surrounding her perfect shape.

Noah and I glance over at each other; he points in my direction. "Looks like you. I think I'm too short to see over the steering wheel. Don't want to run into anything."

I notice the steering wheel, which is about the same height as Noah. He would struggle to peer over. "Ok, but, I know nothing about driving a pirate ship." I toss my arms up in the air.

"Oh, come on. How hard can it be? You just steer in the direction the mermaid princess swims." Noah places his hands on his hips. His shimmery, bare torso flickers back at me in the sunlight.

"Yeah. Easy for you to say. You can just fly."

"I could, but then where would that leave you and Stella? Just behind." He laughs at himself as he takes a seat behind me on the step to the main quarterdeck.

"Ha. Ha. Ha. Very funny." I take hold of the wheel and observe the endless view in front of me. "Aye, aye, Captain Seraphina at your service." I scrunch one side of my face up and seal my other eye shut. "Off to sail the almighty sea." Then, I lean in closer to get a look at that aqua, blue-green tail and hair that takes turns popping up and down out of the water. "I'll just keep following that, and we should be fine, right?" I point to the mermaid.

"Well, good news is I don't think that she can lose us, so let's just hope that all stays status quo and that nothing goes wrong."

"Like what?" I ask, feeling nervous jitters already.

"I don't know...like a bad storm or giant squid attacking us, or something along those lines," Noah says, looking away from me.

"What?" I lose control, stumbling over the steering wheel for a moment. "It doesn't storm in Raiven?" My voice pitches up. "Or does it?"

"Rarely ever. So, let's hope it stays that way," Noah responds.

"And giant squids? Does that even exist here?" My heart races faster.

"Seraphina." Noah pauses. "Everything pretty much exists here." Noah looks off into the distance now, facing the horizon and mermaid. And I really have no other choice but to follow his stare, keeping my eye on the blue-green, bobbing target.

Oh boy. Here we go again. I still feel like throwing up.

CHAPTER TWENTY-ONE

Returning the Rainbow Crystal

AFTER A LONG DAY of sailing and chasing Princess Bella's tail—almost literally—the night has slowly crept upon us. The water realm is such a beautiful, peaceful place. We are lucky enough to catch a view of a family of dolphins swimming, dancing, and soaring in and out of the water, cruising with the pace of the boat.

We even stop at one point at a floating island, to rest up and eat some bananas and coconuts with some small, cute island monkeys. Princess Bella joins in on the fun with us. She comes onto shore, and about ten minutes after drying off in the sun, she grows a pair of legs, which are none-other than perfection—silky white and smooth like the rest of her complexion. But, we know our time has run its course and we're off again to find the invisible door.

So, here we are now floating in the middle of the open salt water, lying down on our backs, watching the moon pretty much take over the whole sky and light it up. All the stars are profound and sparkling in all their glory, looking proud to take up space in its universe as intended. The quietness of the night is serene; and the light sound of the water, making it nothing but pure tranquil. I'm dozing off into a sleep when I'm startled by Princess Bella's voice. "Seraphina, Noah, come here quick and look. You both will want to see this."

We both sprint up and sneak a peek over the pirate ship to get a view of glowing, neon, blue patterns, lighting up a large space of the ocean.

" That's amazing. What is it?" I ask.

"Isn't it? I still can't even get used to it. Their called biolumi-nescent, or glowing plankton," answers the princess, floating with her head just above the water, in the center of all that glowing beauty. She pretty much matches it, hair and all. "They don't do this all the time. But they do it to defend themselves against their predators."

This is one of those moments in time that I want to relish in —a sight that I know I will never forget. *How could I? Wish I had my Smartphone to take a picture.*

But then a loud sound—a rattling sensation—begins taking place. It sounds like a huge train is coming up from underneath us, getting closer and closer. Then, the ship starts swirling around, gaining speed and strength; our ship is in some sort of water tornado that's taking form. Something from underneath of us is causing this extreme force—a funnel that's going to swallow us up.

I scream, "What is happening?"

Noah is trying to brace himself with his arms held out to a tee, and Stella is sliding from one end of the deck to the next, *neighing* and bobbling her head up and down.

Princess Bella leaps into the pits of the water away from this underwater storm and disappears. *Where is she going?* Maybe far away from the trouble I seem to always bring along with me.

Noah becomes a tiny ball of light, flying up and out of the ship. *Oh, just great.* Feeling like I have to now fend for myself, I lie down on the floor—belly down—and clutch a hold around the main mast. I clamp my eyes shut real tight. *This can't be the end—to get this far and it be the end—here. No way.*

As the boat is spinning in an immense circle with the force of the underwater funnel, it feels like it may swallow us up whole, where we will never be found again. A huge, slimy, pink squid jolts out of the water, gripping hold of the ship with two, gigantic tentacles that have sucker-like cups. The squid's strength pulls the ship onto its side, and both Stella and me slide all the way down. It slams me onto my side, causing me to hit my head. I hear a terrorizing sound. *Crunch! Crunch! Crunch!* The ship is breaking, but then, I realize this creature is actually demolishing it with its powerful beak and crushing it with its razor-sharp teeth. As it chomps down, it's getting closer and closer to eating me and Stella alive. I would be its appetizer and Stella the main course. *This can't be happening.*

Chomp, chomp, chomp! It goes to eat and chew us up like a lion ripping and shredding up a zebra, and...*chomp!*

"No!" The word pierces out. I crisscross my arms above my head. "No!"

All of a sudden, the tentacles release the ship. I surrender my arms and run over to the side of the ship to witness the gigantic squid, slithering its body and submerging deep down into the dark ocean, sinking to the bottom. "For crying out loud..."

"Up here." I hear.

I glance up a to a see a small fairy-ball, zipping around my head to turn back into his full form on the boat. "I sprinkled him with just the right amount and type of fairy dust. Put the creature right into a deep sleep." Noah giggles.

The squid isn't the only thing that's sinking into the deep

ocean of the night, so is our ship from the damage the squid did to it.

"This is no laughing matter," I say panicked. "What do we do now?"

"Jump onto my back. I will swim you the rest of the way." It's Princess Bella, bopping her head out of the water's surface beside the ship. She came back.

"Go, Seraphina. I will fly." Noah gestures for me to jump into the water, over to the mermaid.

"What about Stella?" My lower lip starts to tremble.

Stella stands up onto the ship next to me and nestles her nose into my neck, trying to comfort me.

I rub under her chin. "It's ok, girl. I won't leave you."

And just then, Stella kneels down and bows her head. The point of her horn grazes the deck of the ship. A massive, gorgeous rainbow forms out from it, shooting into the dark, starry sky. She shudders her head. Her body, tail, and mane sparkle, and she becomes transparent until she turns into a big ball of glittery dust. A light darts up and shoots over the rainbow into the sky, which then fades away into the distance. *Poof!* She's gone.

My mouth falls open. Noah and Princess Bella are staring off into the sky where nothing now remains, but the twinkling of stars. One, however, is particularly bright and sparkling in all its glory.

Stunned, I realize at that moment, she could have done that anywhere, all along, but chose to never leave my side.

The boat is now sinking even further, deeper into the ocean.

"Hurry, Seraphina. Jump. We don't have any time to think more. I'm sure Stella will find us and come back. Go."

I see the chest with the rainbow crystal inside. It's starting to sink as well. I throw my body in the direction of it, seizing it before it drifts away forever. I fling it open and grab it out just in time. Just after I do, Noah shoves me overboard.

I submerge into the water and come up, gasping for air. Swimming over to Princess Bella, I thrust myself with all of my might over her back. She swims into the distance, away from the sinking ship. The glow of the moon, stars, and rainbow crystal, all in harmony, lead the way.

I'm exhausted, so I rest my head on the back of her shoulder as she carries me through. Noah shines, flying right above us.

I WAKE the next morning on an island with the sun piercing my face. I massage my temples. "Uh, I have such a headache."

"You must be dehydrated. Saltwater air and sun will do that to you." Noah is staring at me, drinking out of a coconut. He hands it to me. "Here, drink it."

I take it from him, *gulping* down the last of it. "Ah." I take a deep breath. Thank you."

"We're here. We've made it to the invisible door." Princess Bella is standing on the island. She is long-legged and barefoot in the white sand.

My attention is then taken by the beauty of the waterfall and rainbow, which overlaps in front of it. "Yes, yes, we've made it." Not wearing my shoes, the warm sand embraces my toes. It's funny to me that how I end is how I started. The beginning of the road, and the end of it, come back around full circle.

Noah flings the pixie dust in the air, which forms the floating door before our eyes. He opens it. But, before we enter through, he bows to Princess Bella, never taking his eyes off of her face. "I can't thank you enough for leading the way and taking us here. I will forever be indebted to you, may you ever need a helping hand or wing." He flutters his wings and grins, pinkish color in his peach face.

She gestures back with a slight bow. "You're welcome. It was the least I can do for both your brave deeds. Thank you."

She walks over to me. Before she can say or do anything, I wrap my arms around her and give her a warm hug.

After we release, Princess Bella positions her hand to her heart, turns around toward the water, and long, pale legs dive back in. Her wet face turns to us. "All of the creatures of Raiven will eternally be grateful." With that, Princess Bella swims away, popping her head out one more time to give her last Miss USA wave before she goes back to her underwater world forever.

NOAH and I now face a cracked, stone spiral staircase that leads up into the blue sky, into purple-white clouds scattered about. *Where does the staircase lead?* I can't see that far into the distance. It's a cloudy mystery. The staircase is intriguing and tempting, calling us to climb it. On both sides, it's surrounded by numerous colorful flowers, including blue hydrangeas, poinsettias, green vines, and many more. There is rich, green grass underneath the start of the staircase, and as it goes along, there's an ocean in the distance. The sound of waves crashes the shore, where the grass meets the sand.

"I guess we should walk up," suggests Noah. He's looking at me with an innocent, little-boy stare that seems just as unsure, yet amused as me.

"I think so too. It's time. But, what about Stella?" I ask, clutching the rainbow crystal as it glows brilliantly—almost like it knows it's close to home.

"She will find her way to us. Have faith." Noah takes the first step.

I follow. We walk side by side up the stairs. As we get higher, a couple of white doves scurry, and then fly away to make room for our approaching steps.

Once we mesh with the clouds and come out the other side, we are greeted by a sight, which only the gods could have created because this place is so blissful that I question if it really is heaven.

A dazzling blue and purple castle engulfs the main view, which reaches so far up into the sky, forming into a light. This light stretches endlessly into the galaxy. It's not night or day, but somehow both. There's a perfect halo of white light that circles around the peak of the castle. Around that light are blotches of pink. Pieces of large rock float around it as well, and white stars sparkle in the blue-black parts of the sky, yet it's not completely dark out; there is still light. I can't explain this phenomenon. The energy field swirls around the castle, and it's so profound that you can't actually see it with the human eye. It looks like a funnel swirl of air, almost like a tornado forming around it, but it's not moving air; it's calm and peaceful. There are massive, ivory statues of angels and fairies that perch themselves on other structures, around the outside of the castle. The green grass and flowers make up the majority of the surrounding ground around it.

This is heaven. It has to be.

We approach the castle, and a golden gate opens up, inviting us in. Standing behind the gate is a giant man, petting a beautiful unicorn. It's Stella. She's standing there with the same man that I saw in my dream the night I fell asleep under the willow tree—my first, out-of-body dream. It's that familiar, old, dark-brown, colored man, wrinkles in his skin, with a long, white beard, holding a large, wooden stick with his perfect, upright posture.

Running over to Stella, I embrace her by wrapping my arms around her neck. She bobs and trills her head, *neighing*. I can feel that she's happy to see me safe as well.

I release my grip from her and observe them both. I swallow hard under a mumble. "Are you Wizard Arbit Maximus?"

He nods ever-so-slightly, but his presence is stronger than any force I've ever been around. Strong and confident, yet he gives off a warm and loving vibe. It feels like being around an old, wise grandpa that you want to hug on a cold night by the fireplace, or like a Santa Claus's lap you want to sit on and tell your Christmas list to. He's that kind of guy, and yet, he's said absolutely nothing.

The rainbow crystal, somewhat to the side, is tucked under my armpit. Wizard Arbit Maximus's eyes view it, and a warm smile caresses his face. His eyes water a bit and tears welt inside of them. They sparkle at me, but never does one tear ever fall. They sit comfortably in the red sockets of his droopy eyes, beyond years. He utters two, simple words and reaches out his arms. "It's home."

"Yes, it is. Where it belongs." I reach out and hand the rainbow crystal back to its owner. Wizard Arbit Maximus obtains what's rightfully his and lifts it in the air to gawk at its glorious colors. It shines bright in his hands and almost blinds me; I duck my head from its brilliance.

This lasts for about a minute, and after it goes back to its normal hue, I look at the wizard still holding it. "I guess it's happy to be back as well." I chuckle.

So does Noah.

"I've been watching you, Seraphina. I have my ways. I know that the wicked witch and most of her trolls are dead. I can't thank you enough for taking on this scary quest for me, for us, for all the living creatures of Raiven. You are a very brave, young girl," the wizard says, smiling at me with a gentle twinkle that comes from his eye.

"You're welcome. And thank you," I respond, and really mean it from the bottom of my heart. "But, can I ask you one thing?"

"What's that?" he replies with a big grin, exposing crooked, big, and yellow-stained teeth.

"How did she do it? How did Alyssa and her trolls steal the rainbow crystal from you in the first place?"

"Oh. That's a long story and one for another time. Plus, you must be exhausted and ready to go home. Let's help get you there." He pats me on the back, then turns and bows toward Noah.

"Sir," Noah bows back at the wizard. "It's an honor."

Wizard Arbit Maximus is distracted by the three-foot, fairy boy, whom he towers over. The wizard examines Noah, but in an admirable way, not intimidating. "You may be small, my dear boy, but your heart and courage are beyond size or measure. Your true character has passed and withstood the test of time."

Noah gradually rolls himself up from his bow. He nods his head at the wizard, acknowledging him, but by the look on Noah's face, you can see that he has never been paid such a compliment from such a commendable individual.

"You are a great warrior. I will tell your queen. She will be very proud, and you will be highly rewarded."

"Thank you, sir." He bows again, staying like that for some time.

I know in my heart that Noah has received the ultimate validation. A real warrior fairy has been seen and acknowledged for his efforts. There is no higher reward than that for a fairy. He has become my newest, yet dearest friend of all time. And I know now what is really important to him. *Besides, isn't that what friends are for? To be eternally connected...to know what's most important to them, or what they need and when they need it most? At least, that is what I've learned along the way.*

"And you—" his old, wise eyes glare into my soul— "have saved Raiven, and Earth." His voice is deep and raspy. "Without Raiven, there would be no Earth. You see, Seraphina, we are all connected. Everything has a purpose, and without one single flower, bee, fairy, butterfly, or human, we would all cease to exist. We are all fulfilling it with every breath that we take, working for the betterment of our planet—our world." His large, chocolate arms and hands stretch out wide, stick still in hand. "And what a wonderful world it is."

"I didn't realize before that this was ever here, though. Why not? Why don't more humans know about Raiven?"

"The species of our world is making Earth better every day, but humans don't even realize it. Every plant has an elf who oversees its growth, and all of nature is in perfect harmony cause of our fairies who look over it." He points at Noah with his stick.

"I know. I see that," I say. "But I want all the other humans to see what I see."

"Did you know that two people can't see the same rainbow in exactly the same way? Do you know why that is?"

I shrug my shoulders. "No. I don't know."

"Because it's viewed only from a very certain angle relative to the sun's rays, so maybe while one may feel under or at the end of a rainbow, the other may be further off a bit. So, it will be seen differently be every other person observing it. However, it's still there."

Still confused by what he's trying to say, I give a cheesy thumbs up.

"Why can one see it, while the other can't? Think, Seraphina. *Both* the rain and sun need to be present to make a rainbow appear. And it's just an object that can't be approached...unless—" he pauses.

"Unless?" I really think about this, looking from right to left as if the answers are there in front of me.

There's a moment of silence.

"Unless—" the wizard whispers, — "they're ready to see it. Every person perceives everything differently."

Another brief moment of silence lingers. Then, it hits me like a ton of bricks. "Unless, there's hope?" My voice pitches high when I say the word *hope*. It's a question, but not. I know the answer. "You have to go through the rain, before you can get to the rainbow. It took me losing my best friend to see Raiven."

"Yes." The wizard squeezes his hand and makes a fist like a teacher when his student wins the spelling bee.

"I was hopeless before I came, but I never completely gave up. I had hope in my heart that I would see her again someday. And, and, I did. That's why I was the chosen one. All the fates completely aligned for me...for me to have...to have faith. Just because we can't always see what's not in front of us, doesn't mean that it's not there."

"And one can see a rainbow anytime they choose," Wizard Arbit Maximus says. "They just have to be ready for it, to see it with their heart first." He places his hands over his heart.

"Amazing." I pace.

At that moment, from a distance, a multi-colored butterfly approaches, flapping its wings toward us. As it gets closer, I recognize it. It's Sebastian. My heart races with excitement.

"Are you ready to go home now, Seraphina?" The clever wizard asks me. "Sebastian is ready to take you back."

"I am, but what about—" I peer at her, "—Stella?" I caress her between her eyes with my forehead.

"Stella will be safe here with me and the crystal in our castle. She's meant to be here, with us, to protect and to ride with me when I need her. But, because of you, you birthed her, so she will eternally be connected to your soul. You both will be able to feel each other whenever you need." Wizard Arbit Maximus's smile is reassuring.

"How do I say goodbye?" My lip quivers. "To Stella? To Noah? How? I can't." I force the lump down my throat.

"You don't. We will always be a part of your heart. Just like Josie Lee, who is guiding you, so will we. Plus, there is no such thing as goodbye." The wizard's smile forms a faint, long line on his face, and he tilts his head.

Sebastian anxiously flutters his wings around my upper-body. "See, see, see. I told you, didn't I?"

I crack a grin. "Yes, Sebastian, you told me. You were right." My grin becomes bigger and brighter, and I bat my eyes at him. "It's nice to see you again."

"Ready when you are to take you back now to where you belong. I'm sure you miss your family." Sebastian swirls around my head.

I rest my hands over my heart. "I do, terribly."

"Once you step inside my castle, there is an entrance way back into the travel vortex. It will take you right back through, down and out back to that large, wooden door, which you originally entered through. It's a bit of a shortcut. You will then be back into the forest and on your way home." The wizard guides me by the small of my back to lead the way.

I can't help but lose it, and begin the hard, ugly cry. Whipping around and dropping to my knees, I grasp my arms around Noah, squeezing the breath out of him. "I'm going to miss you so much. Thank you. Thank you for sticking to your promise and never giving up on me, not for even one moment. You are my new, best friend."

Noah snuggles his face in my neck, through my hair. He has whatever part of his arms he can manage to get around me and squeezes me back. "I will miss you too. But, I promise, one day, somehow, we will meet again. I've been with you in this life and lifetimes before. I'm not going anywhere. You just take care of yourself. And you never know? I just may peek in on you from time to time." He chuckles.

I lay one small kiss goodbye on his cheek, and he returns the motion, leaving me with a warm smirk. "Goodbye...for now."

"Goodbye," I say.

Stella nods her head swiftly. *Neigh...neigh...neigh!* She licks my tears and then snorts a big breath out of her nose, which blows a *swish* of air, rustling up my hair. I squint my eyes from the forceful spray.

"Stop, Stella. Don't make it any harder than it already is for me. Just know that I love you, and you'll always be a part of me." I brush the side of her face, feeling her white, silky fur for the last time. "Bye, girl."

And with those words, one tear collapses in slow motion from Stella's eye to the ground. It's colorful, like a rainbow, but before it hits the ground, it turns into a dust of glowing, glittering light. The light swirls in the air, forming a star, transcending into an energy field that shoots into the dark sky, perching itself there in one particular spot. It twinkles brighter than any other star in the sky. We all look up, viewing it. I gasp. "Whoa."

"That star shines for the both of you. She wants you to know. As long as your souls exist together, so will the star." Wizard Arbit Maximus informs me, both of us now looking up. "And anytime you want to talk to her, you just talk to that star and make a wish, and she will hear your dreams and see into your heart. Stella will answer you, but you must be paying attention in order to know how she answers."

"How will I know?" I ask, drying my tears away with the back of my hand.

"Oh, you'll know. You'll get signs." The wizard beams, which forms even more wrinkles upon his old, brown face.

"Goodbye," I say to the wizard and shake his large hand. "Thank you for everything. And please say goodbye and thank you to Queen Ivy for me as well."

I step inside the wizard's castle; blue and purple, sparkly stone covers the walls and floor. The space inside pretty much consists of ancient furniture, statues, and a massive library of shelves of book after book. In addition, there inside waiting for me, is that invisible door (floating effortlessly in mid-air), which appears at this moment. I glide over to it and climb inside. Sebastian flies beside me. Twisting around one last time to get a vision of the faces of my dear friends—Noah, Stella, and the wizard—I feel that familiar twinge in my belly. I hate to leave them, but I'm anxious to get back home to continue on with my life where I left off. However, I will never lose hope that one day I will be seeing all of their faces again. With one hand over my belly, I use the other to wave goodbye. For the last time on my adventure through Raiven, I cross over inside the invisible door.

I glide down the vortex through a spiral slide that connects all the realms. This time, I can see all the colors changing in front of my eyes as I pass through each one—first violet, then blue, green, yellow, orange, and even some shades of red—until I pop out through to the rich grass of Fairyland, standing in front of that recognizable, wooden door. I'm right at the same entrance I started.

"Go ahead, knock three times again," Sebastian murmurs in my ear, while his wings flutter in mid-air.

Knock, knock, knock. A pause. Then, the large door slowly *creaks* open.

Walking through, back out to the other side, I notice the same leprechaun, sitting guard by his pot of gold. He tips his top hat at me. "Later, me lass. And a we' mighty thank ya'."

"Um, you're welcome." I give him a slight wave goodbye, and I continue walking away from the leprechaun, the pot of gold, brilliant rainbow, and world of Raiven.

Looking at the little butterfly who started it all, I wave. "Goodbye, Sebastian." A tear rolls down my cheek.

"No. No. No. I can't. You know what I hate more than crying? Goodbyes. I'll just say, 'til' we meet again." He takes one big *sniffle* through his tiny body, and Sebastian flies and swoops back around away forever.

'Til we meet again, little friend.

I'm back in the forest where I first encountered Sebastian on that gloomy day. But, wait, it still is that same gloomy day, because no time has changed. It's even still wet outside, and so am I in the same wet clothes. I'm what's changed. I feel lighter, better, more mature, braver even, and of course, more hopeful than I've felt in my entire life. I know now what I didn't know then — that the journey doesn't end here, and it didn't end there in Raiven either. I will see all of my friends again one day when the time is right, because in actuality, there is no end.

CHAPTER TWENTY-TWO

Home Sweet Home

DARTING through the front door of my house, I swing it open so hard that it *slams* the wall of the outside making a big *boom*. "Mom, Mom, where are you?" I shout.

Dinner is cooking. It smells like spaghetti and meatballs—a favorite in our house. *Mmm, even smells like home.*

"Honey, I'm here in the kitchen," I hear my mom say from the other room.

I run into the kitchen and throw my arms around my mom, squeezing the air out of her.

"Honey. What's wrong?" my mom asks. She looks at me all wet from the rain, even though it didn't rain, but did, or whatever. That time thing still gets me all confused. "You're wet. Go change. You'll catch a cold," my mom orders.

"I don't understand what's gotten into you. Did you not take the bus and walk home? Are you crazy?"

I avoid that question like a person with the flu. "No, I just want to stay here, hugging you for a moment. I missed you;

that's all." I gaze into my mom's eyes, really taking it in, forgetting how pretty she is. She doesn't look her age of forty-eight. People never get it right. My mom loves that; she just has a young spirit about her.

"Ahhh, honey, you just went to school for the day, but I missed you too. Glad you're home safe and sound." My mom kisses the top of my head while stirring the tomato sauce with a wooden spoon.

"Oh, me too. Me too. I love you, Mom."

"Oh, honey," my mom drops the spoon and squeezes me. "I love you *more*."

"I'm sorry if I've been mean to you and dad since we moved here, but I promise, I never will be again."

"Are you sure you're ok?" My mom examines my face.

"Oh, Mom, I'm better than ok. You have no idea." I squeeze her back even tighter.

A COUPLE MONTHS HAVE PASSED. I take a walk by myself to the park in my back yard where I first met Josie Lee. It's now spring, and there's a crisp, cool breeze outside. I see a bench and walk over to it and sit down. Gazing out at the nature around me, I remember my journey through Raiven and all my great friends that I met along the way—Noah, Stella, Sebastian, the elves and dragons, Princess Bella, the wizard; I miss them all.

Everything has been going pretty good with school. I'm really enjoying fifth grade, and I love my new teacher, Mrs. Adams. I have been hanging around a new, fun circle of friends; the girls at my school are nice. No one has replaced Josie Lee, but that's ok, because no one ever will. No word has dared been uttered from my mouth about my experience; they'd never believe it anyway. *Maybe I'll meet someone one day I can tell, or even who can go there with me? That would be a very special person. That's silly.* I laugh with the thought. Every now and then, I get the urge to tell my parents, but I know they'd think I was crazy and probably put me in therapy. So, for now, the secret stays with me and all is well that way. *I'm happy.* However, sometimes I still have to ask myself if it all was just a dream.

I get up from the bench. Walking with my hands in the pockets of my skinny, ripped jeans,I glance down. I realize that I'm wearing the same jeans that I wore the day I ventured into the magical world of Raiven.

I feel something almost sandy-like inside one of the pockets. With those thoughts still fresh in my mind, I pull out of it a handful of pixie dust, glittering and sparkling in the sun. It must have gotten stuck in there one of the times that Noah sprinkled me with it. *Who knows, really? Magic. And then it strikes me. A dream? Nah. It was more real and alive than anything I've ever experienced in my life.*

Just then from my side vision, I catch a three-foot shadow shift behind a tree from a distance, and I'm left with the strong aroma of gardenias; I can't help but grin from ear to ear.

ABOUT THE AUTHOR

Samantha graduated with a BS in Journalism from Florida International University in 2003. She wrote and reported entertainment scripts that were aired on FOX WSVN 7 in Miami, FL and OWL Radio at Florida Atlantic University in Boca.

Samantha has always been passionate about writing and has been writing short stories and poetry for as long as she can remember. She began writing children's stories in 2004 and even wrote and finished a screenplay. In addition to RAINBOW CRYSTAL, she completed a 18,000 humorous, animal-talking, chapter book called MURPHY: THE PHAT CAT. Her 136-page screenplay is based on a true story about her Italian great-grandparents and is currently being shopped in Hollywood.

Samantha is also the VP/Director of PR for a charity called *Rainbow Guardian*, which serves the intellectually challenged/developmentally disabled population, including autism. Mainly, she's a busy-bee being a wife to Richard and mother to their children, Bella and Lorenzo. You can also find her enjoying reading, working out, blogging, baking, spending quality time with good friends, and/or traveling, whenever she can find extra time (usually one of those activities accompanies a cup of coffee or glass of wine), minus the working out part. However, there are always exceptions. Samantha also has three bulldogs and one white, fluffy cat named Gracie. She's the princess of the house. She has a lot of love around her and feels very blessed every day.

www.cleanreads.com

CPSIA information can be obtained
at www.ICGtesting.com
Printed in the USA
FSHW02n2335300918
52481FS